LOOSE COINS

LOOSE
COINS

Joe L. Hensley and Guy M. Townsend

ST. MARTIN'S PRESS ☙ NEW YORK

Library of Congress Cataloging-in-Publication Data

Hensley, Joe L., date
    Loose coins / by Joe L. Hensley and Guy M. Townsend. — 1st ed.
        p.   cm.
    ISBN 0–312–19297–5
    I. Townsend, Guy M.   II. Title.
    PS3558.E55L66   1998
    813'.54—dc21   98–21126

First Edition: November 1998

10 9 8 7 6 5 4 3 2 1

LOOSE COINS

I

Thursday, July 18, 9:30 P.M.

I'D PLAYED A few times before in the Thursday night poker game in the apartment above Ralph's Coin Shop. It wasn't for me a big game. Once I'd played in fifty-dollar ante no limit games, but that had been during sweet Judy time, before she divorced me, and before I was suspended from the practice of law by the Tennessee State Bar disciplinary people. Those big games had been when the money was piling up in dirty sheafs, money that had no meaning to me then, like a kid's Monopoly holdings.

Ralph's game was dollar ante and half the pot limit, high stakes for me now. With six players you could open for three bucks, raise more, and progress up from there. Most late bets were in the five to twenty dollar range. Stiff enough.

Ralph's Coin Shop was on Highland, near Memphis State University. When I got asked to fill a poker chair I filled it. I owed Ralph. He'd offered me a job and a place to be when no one else cared. He'd taken a chance and trusted me when he saw I was sober and working hard to stay that way.

Ralph had done up his upstairs elaborately. There was a wet bar and there were deep leather couches and chairs. There was a professional-style fold up poker table with pullouts for glasses and recessed places in front of every player to hold chips and money.

I knew all the other players. Two of them I knew a little, three I knew pretty well. The two vague ones were a pair nicknamed "Ace" and "Deuce" who offered a bimonthly mail-bid coin sale out of a Memphis post office box and who were constant, querulous visitors at area coin shops. I knew them from Ralph's coin shop where I'd been designated to both "watch them," and to "wait on them." Most of my previous discussions with them had been coin talk. Ace was tall, thin, and high thirtyish with a bald spot in suspiciously black hair. He was a mostly silent man with quick, sometimes angry eyes. His favorite expression, once I'd named a price, was "Jesus, that much?" Deuce was maybe ten years older. He was short and he smiled meaninglessly a lot, camouflaging himself from the world. Ralph claimed Deuce was a good coin grader, but Deuce's nose looked more like he was a whisky expert than a coin expert to me.

Ralph Shedden, my now part-time employer, part-time landlord, was a fanatic card player. Since his wife had died a year or so back his two remaining joys were running his coin shop and playing poker. He was an honest, sixtyish man who hated anyone thinking he'd ever done a charitable thing. His business prospered. I'd known him for years. I'd bought some good, rare things from him, early large cents, high-grade type coins, back when I could afford them. I knew that Judy had sold some of the pieces back to him after she'd been awarded them in our divorce.

I also knew well John Wayne "Duke" Theotokopolis. I'd defended him on a tax-fraud charge in federal court toward the end of my legal career. I'd kept him out of jail, but it literally cost him a lockbox full of coins he'd had to walk away from. He was deeply into coins then. He was youngish, less than forty, and one sharp dude. He'd done what I advised when I'd represented him, even when it meant ignoring about a million lockbox dollars. I thought it possible the IRS boys might still be watching that anonymously held box, waiting like a black widow spider for someone in an Oxford suit to come calling. Staying away had likely kept Duke out of federal prison.

I wondered, looking him over, why he bothered to play. The

game had to be penny ante for him. Maybe he played for the same reason I did, for Ralph. When he'd been buying coins, and he'd specialized in gold with kings on the obverse, he'd bought those coins from Ralph. He'd liked bulk gold, coins that sold near the raw gold price. But six months before I'd given up drinking I knew he'd given up coin collecting. He'd sold what remained (outside the forbidden lockbox) of his collection back to Ralph and I'd not seen him around the shop since I'd been in it.

The final well-known face was a black one: Harlan Roberts, retired police captain, having done his twenty-plus on the Memphis force before going on to other, larger things. Now he ran a guard agency and probably made half-a-dozen times what he'd once made as a cop. Ralph saved rare U.S. currency and Nationals for a first look by Harlan. I liked Harlan. I'd liked him before I was suspended from law practice and I liked him now. Sometimes, before my suspension, I'd not believed he liked me much, but that was all right. My job then had been getting out the people he'd put in, and I'd been good at the job. Now he was easier with me and liked to kid me about being a "tough private eye." I'm not.

And so we played poker. Tonight it was mostly six and seven card stud, no wild cards, no high-low splits, just plain, tough poker. It was a tight and semisilent game. I'd been winning some and losing some.

There were two entry doors into Ralph's. One led down to the shop below, the other opened to rickety steps up from the alley.

Maybe the intruder had seen the cars parked back behind the shop and guessed what was happening. Maybe he'd watched before. Or maybe someone had talked in the wrong place about the game and he'd heard and waited for this right time.

Those were my first thoughts.

Maybe.

He was a lone robber unless someone waited and watched outside. He kicked in the old door above the alley and stood briefly in the doorway, shotgun in hand, wheeling it back and

3

forth, taking deadly command. He eyed the small piles of money on the table through the eye slit in his ski mask.

"Freeze, if you want to live," he said contemptuously. "I'll take all that," he added. He aimed the shotgun in my general direction. "Gather it up for me now, Al. Quickly, quickly." His voice was harsh and I saw that his pupils were tiny. It came to me that he was on something, heroin maybe, or strong hash. *And he knew my name.*

I got up submissively. The others sat quietly and without protest. I collected their piles of money, maybe totaling a couple of thousand for all the players. I carried the resulting stack gingerly and with no quick moves. The gun followed me, its barrel opening huge. The robber's finger stayed on the trigger, tightening, then relaxing.

Sweat ran down my back.

"You're coming with me when I leave, Al," the bandit said softly. "You and me and old man Ralph will leave together. We're going to take the inside stairs to the shop below where I've got a few good gold coins spotted. With the two of you helping me out of town maybe these others will be smart enough not to call any law."

"Yes sir," I said. I nodded quickly, almost groveling in front of him. I could see that he'd dismissed me as a force.

The whole thing was wrong. He knew me. He also knew Ralph. I probably wasn't the best one to take as a hostage, but he'd picked me out first. I was scared.

There were guns in the coin shop, a revolver behind the big case, a .45 automatic hidden under papers in a desk drawer. I remembered that. But if he knew the shop, Ralph, and me, he might also know about the guns.

"Get up now, Ralph," the robber ordered. "I want you to walk careful over here toward me. Stand with Al. Slow and easy does it."

Without moving my head I could see Ralph out of the corner of my eye. He got up slowly. The gun went his way, perhaps to speed action.

4

I was near the robber. I was still bent and submissive. I held out the sheaf of money imploringly and that brought the gun partway back to me. Half between, when he started another trajectory back to Ralph, I threw the wad of money hard into the air and dived recklessly at the robber's legs. I rolled them out from under him. He cursed and tried to avoid me, to leap upward and retain his balance. At the same time the gun returned to bear on where I'd been, but now I was under him and that gun. I looked up and saw surprise in his eyes. He managed to fire one shell and I felt the heat of the blast as buckshot went past my legs and into the floor. I kept looking up and watching his angry, startled eyes. Suddenly they were unseeing and dead. He fell over me and I crawled out from under. Duke Theotokopolis had a small derringer halfway out. I'd never known he was into carrying guns. Harlan Roberts held a large, smoking automatic. I did know he went armed and had gambled he carried a gun all the time. I didn't remember hearing any shots other than the single blast of the shotgun, but the robber was facedown, motionless, and there was a lot of blood coming from two holes, fore and aft, in his head.

I was unscathed.

"You okay?" Harlan asked. His dark face was expressionless. It was a question only. I didn't think it made much difference to him what I answered.

"I guess I am."

"If you hadn't rolled him I might never have gotten a chance at him," Harlan said evenly. He looked me over, now mildly curious. "Why'd you risk it?"

I shrugged. "He wanted into the shop. And he wanted to take Ralph and me along with him. I got a look at his eyes and he was high on coke or heroin. I figured there was a chance we might not get back from his planned trip. And I remembered you always carried a gun. I've never seen you without one."

"You were right on that. I always carry it."

"It seemed better odds than going with him."

Harlan nodded. "There's always the chance that a hostage

taker is only delaying his executions to a more convenient place. You did okay for a reformed drunk. Very quick." He looked over at Ralph who shivered in his chair. "Raise Al's pay or cut his rent, Ralphie. He may just have saved your skinflint butt." He shook his head curiously. "And made me decide he's a little bit smarter and tougher than I'd believed before."

"What happens now?" Duke asked. "Do we call anyone?"

"You bet your Greek ass we do," Harlan said. "The first thing to do is put the cards away, fold this card table back over against the wall where Ralph keeps it when it's not in action, and then everyone fixes a drink except Al." He looked at me and grinned. "You can have another Diet Pepsi, Al, with or without caffeine."

"The very thing I need," I said. I was shaking by now also. I wanted a real drink badly, but not enough to retreat back down into the dark world where once I'd existed. Not ever again.

"It was just a summer night get-together, a few friendly drinks, some talk, coin pals kind of thing. This deadbutt came in to rob us and also to hit Ralph's coin shop below," Harlan continued. He turned to Ralph. "Light up your teevee, Ralph. Use up a little wattage. Get us a ball game or some kind of war movie."

"They'll know what we were doing," Ralph said. "They'll figure it out."

Harlan nodded. "Poker ain't a hell of a big local sin, Ralph. Besides knowing and proving are different things. Ask your boy Al sometime about how that works. He used to be an expert in the area. Don't worry about any lies we tell tonight. I'll tell the boys downtown the truth about what we were doing later, but not tonight. Tomorrow I'll talk to someone up the chain in the department and cut off further inquiry there." He stepped forward and foot-turned the robber over roughly, then bent and stripped the concealing bloody mask away. The face revealed was white, anonymous, thirtyish, substantially out of focus from taking two heavy caliber slugs through the head, and unknown to me.

"Anyone know this guy because he sure don't look familiar to me?"

Four people shook their heads, including me. Ralph Shedden didn't.

"You know him, Ralphie?" Harlan asked.

"Maybe I've seen him before. In the shop or somewhere. And he knew me."

"Correction," Harlan said. "He knew you and Al."

"He might have seen me in the coin shop if that's where Ralph saw him," I said. "It gets busy and I don't try to look at everyone. Ralph, being the owner, looks closer." I work the counter for Ralph when I'm not working outside of the shop.

Harlan went expertly through pockets, but there was not a lot to be found. An open pack of Kools, half gone, some matches without an advertisement. A roll of small denomination bills with a rubber band around them. Two small keys on a chain.

Car keys?

"See if there's a strange car parked out back?" Harlan said to me.

I went to the broken door and out it. I reached back in and turned on Ralph's outer floodlight.

There were cars below, but they were identifiable. Ralph's car, my VW, and an old Ford Crown Vic that belonged to Ace and Deuce. I'd seen it parked in front of the shop before. Harlan's new-looking Audi was the class of the crowd. Duke's Lincoln Mark, which I'd seen before, wasn't present.

I shook my head at Harlan when I returned from the outside. I looked at Duke Theotokopolis. "How'd you get here, Duke?"

"Cab. I don't drink and drive these days." He smiled. "That's smarter than either of us used to be."

"How about our money?" Ace asked, looking at the fallen currency.

"Leave it beside him for now," Harlan ordered. "Once they see what's happened they'll maybe let us pick it up. I would." He smiled showing white teeth. "Dead buddy here, he won't complain." His eyes moved to me, contemplative again. "You sure moved good, Al. It was something I never expected out of you, but I wasn't so surprised that I had problems getting my gun out. Maybe you'll make a better private investigator than you did

7

a lawyer if you can stay off the booze. But you better start carrying a gun."

"Never could handle one. I'd blow my own foot off," I said. I was beginning to feel a little better. "Or blow the world's head off."

"I'll teach you a foolproof way to shoot one day," Harlan said, smiling. "Might come in handy for you in your new business."

"You ought to see Al on them rings and bars and gymnasium horses," Ralph said, regaining some animation. "He can do almost anything. Just like them crazy athletes on TV."

"You into gymnastics, Al?" Harlan asked.

"Once I was. I work out some now is all. Just exercise."

THE POLICE CAME and were with us for a time. A patrol car arrived first, then two homicide detectives, one black, one white. I knew the black one a little from my time as a lawyer. He nodded at me, but was more interested in Harlan.

"What were you doing here, Captain?"

"*Retired* Captain, Smitty," Harlan corrected, his voice light and bantering. "Having a sociable drink or two. Talking some coins. We were even thinking about playing some friendly poker when the door broke in and our newcomer on the floor tried to rob us." He considered the body on the floor.

Smitty nodded, his dark eyes wise. "Sure, that's it. That's just exactly what you all were doing." He grinned and Harlan grinned back, everything friendly.

"You shoot him, Al?" the black detective asked me. "I heard it said around, back the line, that you went to the clerk's office and bought yourself a private investigator's ticket."

"Not him, Smitty," Harlan said. "I confess. I'm your man. I shot the bastard. But Al made it possible. He tackled him when the dead dude was covering him with a shotgun."

Smitty shrugged amiably, not caring. He leaned down and looked at the dead face of the intruder. He whistled a tuneless song. He straightened up after a while and shook his head.

"I think maybe all of you were very damned lucky. If this guy's who I think then he's a professional hunter."

"A contract pro?" Harlan asked, surprised.

"Strictly pro," Smitty answered. "Name's Shell or Shelly or something. He was in town once before and I saw him. That was maybe three or four years back. I was part of a team that picked him up at the airport after someone took out State Senator Dealman. Remember that one, Harlan? Done neat and sweet. Dealman sold out up front and then reneged on a vote. He got a final payment of a single shot in the right eye with a .22. Dead man here was clean at the airport and there weren't any witnesses, nothing to hold him on. But this is the same lad." He shook his head. "He'd not be in town just to be doing a simple robbery."

Harlan shook his head. "He came in with a shotgun. He talked hard and got Al to collect our money. Then he was going to take Ralph and Al with him after he took what he wanted from the coin place downstairs. Al got ambitious and took his legs out from under him like some all-pro tackle. I shot him in the confusion."

"Did he know anyone?"

"He called Ralph and Al by name."

Smitty looked at Ralph and then, longer, at me. "Either of you got anything bad going? Maybe someone out there in Memphis town mad enough at you to shoot your sporting equipment off?"

Ralph shook his head.

"I've not done anything that would make anyone want to shoot me," he said.

I nodded slowly.

"You don't look sure," Smitty said mildly.

I nodded a little harder to reinforce things, but I had a problem. I wasn't sure. I'd represented a lot of bad people back the years. Some of them I'd won for, but I'd lost a lot of cases also. Criminal lawyers don't win them all. I'd been threatened dozens of times. It was possible that someone might have contracted with the man on the floor for my life. He'd singled me out from the crowd first. I'd lived a long time in an alcohol fog. I didn't

even remember some of the enemies I undoubtedly had. It was something to worry on.

"Might be he was just down on his luck," Harlan said. "It went down like a robbery."

Smitty shrugged. "Maybe." He looked around the room and spotted Duke Theotokopolis sprawled in an easy chair.

"What's a high roller like you doing here, Duke?"

"Spending an evening with old friends," Duke said. "I used to buy me some coins through Ralph. And Al was once my lawyer." He stopped as if was aware he'd said more than he needed to say. He leaned back.

"If it wasn't for Captain Harlan being here," Smitty said, smile reappearing, "I might just tote you all downtown and we'd talk a lot more and very late at my place trying to make some sense of this." He shrugged. "But for today I'm going to write it up like the captain tells it. I don't like it lots, but that's how it'll be." He winked solemnly at Harlan, excluding him from his suspicions.

A police photographer took some photos and the body was removed, leaving only the blood stains of the robber.

We amicably split up the money and silently ended the evening.

We used the back steps to the street. In the parking area below Harlan whacked me on the back.

"Saved our butts, you did," he said, still not believing it.

I HAD A small apartment off Monroe, near Christian Brothers College. I drove my elderly Dasher there. The car was the leavings of my marriage with Judy, my divorce dowry. She'd taken the almost-new Mercedes, what was left of my coins (I'd sold a lot of them in a final drinking-gambling splurge), and the furniture. Even so it hadn't been the evenest of splits for her. I figured in that last year plus, after the money had slowed to a trickle from legal clients who'd heard I had both drinking and disciplinary problems, that I'd gone through most of what had been accumulated. It had been a long, sick party.

The Dasher needed points and plugs. It sputtered up into the drive and I parked in a central lot in a spot bearing my apartment number. People splashed in the apartment pool. Someone female and friendly waved to me from the blue, floodlighted water. I waved back. Flowers were in bloom and the world around me smelled good. And I was sober.

I walked up steps and keyed my door. Inside my place I got a Diet Pepsi and poured it over ice. I turned my lights out and sat in the window recess and watched the late-night swimmers. The crowd was male and female, mostly young, probably lonely. I'd been to the pool a few times.

I reviewed my life a little.

I did it mostly because I thought it was me the man with the contract to kill had come calling for.

Me.

2

Thursday, July 18, 11:45 p.m.

MY FULL NAME is Allan Loomis Sears, Al Sears. The Loomis comes from my great-grandfather on my mother's side of the family. He won a Medal of Honor in World War One and became famous because of it, a poor man's Sergeant York. My father told me that great-grampaw onced confessed to him that he'd been in the right place at the right time and some general had happened to see his foolish behavior.

I graduated Summa Cum Laude from Memphis State law school ten years back. I'd gone there after four years at Tennessee, where I'd majored in business (accounting) and been enough of a gymnast to make the Olympic squad of the era, but not good enough to win a medal.

I didn't despair about the lost Olympic medal for long because I had the world by the throat and doing whatever I decreed by the time I got out of law school. I had job offers from all over, Washington, New York, Chicago, but I'd also captured a gorgeous Memphis belle, then Judy Barnes, who finished her sophomore year in undergraduate school the year I graduated from law school.

I decided home was where the heart was and so I stayed in Memphis to protect my interests. I went to work for a good local firm and they pushed me along hard. I made a name for myself early on with them. I worked hard and kept up with advance sheets and seminars. I became a second-class, first-rate trial lawyer, flamboyant and cocky. There were many things I didn't know about jury trials, but there were lots of things I did know. I had an instinct for courtroom games and a knack for going for police and prosecutorial jugulars. A certain element of society loved me for it. I defended burglars, con men, thieves, robbers, and a dozen murderers.

I married Judy in the June after her graduation from Memphis State. It was one of *the* weddings of the year. Now, when I think on it, maybe that was a main reason why we did marry. It was the expected thing. We were both into expected things then. She was old Memphis, not huge money, but lots of family name and dozens of haughty relatives. She was bright and beautiful. She was ambitious for both of us. She took a proffered job with one of the local television stations. At first she did specials for them. Then she moved up and become part of the evening news. She came over the tube as lovely, warm, and earnest. Soon she anchored the evening news and Memphis was in love with her.

The job kept her busy. My evening contacts with her became watching her report the undoings at city hall or describe the latest fire or strike.

The marriage went quickly wrong, but we stuck with it until we'd wrung it dry. She was away a lot, working and playing. I was away a lot, working and drinking. Dealing with scum all day gave me a thirst. I drank. I drank a lot.

My tough, aggressive firm kept smelling my breath and seeing my bloodshot eyes and decided they could make do without me. Stung, I opened my own office and took some of their best clients with me.

I kept drinking. Things got worse.

Judy took a job in Chicago. *Moving up.*

We argued hotly about her taking the job. I ordered her not to take it. She took it and I went on a blast. I stayed blasted for a long, expensive time.

I missed office appointments and failed to show for court dates. I drank. I drank mornings, afternoons, and nights. I started early with Bloodies or screwdrivers and continued with martinis and straight scotches. My excuse was I was mourning Judy. I realize now that if Judy had been sweet and submissive I'd have found other reasons to drink.

I was protected for a time. I was good at the business. Prosecutors agreed to continuances, judges granted more time, but no one lasts forever when the bottle replaces writs, motions, and picking juries.

One day, not long back, I got suspended for three years. The order came two days after Judy got her noncontested divorce.

I did one semibright thing about then. The day after my suspension came I went to the County Clerk's office and applied for a private investigator's license. I fit within the statute. I was twenty-one years of age or older, no longer excluded because I was a "practicing" lawyer. I had the seventy dollars to pay, and the investigation by the district attorney general indicated I had no felony or misdemeanor arrests in any state or federal court. Whoever did the investigation (if anyone actually did) perhaps ignored the "good moral character" part, or didn't know me that well.

I spent more time in bottle battle. During that time my identification card came and got deposited with other unneeded stuff on my dresser.

I found the bottom of the world.

Then, one day, I quit.

I didn't have AA, although it was strong in Memphis, available, useful, and had worked for others. I quit cold turkey on my own. The closest of my surviving relatives was two hundred miles away and knew only enough to be scandalized by my drinking. We'd mutually ignored each other for a long time. I had no church and almost no friends. Except I had a "kind of" friend in Ralph.

Perhaps I quit for *me*.

I quit because I no longer liked being a drunk.

• • •

I DIDN'T LIKE the idea of being dead either. I'd come close at the poker game. I couldn't wash it out of my thoughts that the man had come to Ralph's place for more than cash and coins. The guy had known me, known Ralph. He'd parked a car someplace, hence the keys found in his pocket, then bussed or taxied in, likely intending to use a car of ours for his escape. And Smitty had said he thought the man was a contract killer.

Maybe he had come for Ralph. Maybe also the two of us were only pawns and he'd intended to kill someone else before we left, like Duke or Harlan. *But he'd known me and known Ralph.*

It was possible someone out of my past hated me enough to pay for my death. A lot of people might be pleased to read of my death in an obituary column. I wondered if any of those would pay execution fees to see such a notice. Someone who'd come into money? Someone, maybe, who'd finally decided I must die?

It could be someone else the killer had wanted.

Harlan Roberts had probably made his share of enemies during his police years. Duke Theotokopolis had gang connections and was as shady as a July tree. Ace and Deuce seemed small potatoes, but I needed to verify that. I knew they'd steal. They had from Ralph. Maybe they'd stolen big from the wrong person.

I still believed it was me. The thing to do was check them all out, look until I found an answer.

I finished what was left of the Pepsi I'd opened. It had gone flat and watery. I sat the glass on a week-old *Time* magazine that lay on the end table by my window. I gazed out at the diminishing crowd of night swimmers. Soon, down at the pool, they'd either pair off or give it up. Probably lonely either way.

I thought about Ralph Shedden because I owed him.

I started buying coins from him after law school. I first bought a bright 1907 Indian head cent for a lucky piece, then decided that the one penny needed a good fortune companion. Owning two got me interested in the series. I put the set together. I moved on from Indians to other coppers. I read coin books and subscribed to *Numismatic News* and *Coin World*.

With big money coming in I'd bought a double pot full of coins, mostly copper, mostly from Ralph.

Our friendship had moved a step beyond dealer-customer before my drinking made me forget buying coins.

Ralph's wife died about the same time Judy bailed out of the game for Chicago.

Ralph withdrew into himself. I didn't much notice because I was seeing little but the bottle. I sold the coins back to Ralph. He bought them without interest, but he paid for them fairly.

When Judy got the divorce and I got suspended I heard she sold what remained of the coins to Ralph. She'd been in his shop with me in good days and it was a place she knew, a place where she'd learned to exclaim smilingly over the astonishing prices I paid for coins.

When Judy approached Ralph about selling the coins he'd phoned me to make certain it was all right, that they were hers to sell. That had been in prime alcoholic time. I vaguely recalled later having been abusive of both Judy and Ralph and making an impossible suggestion as to what he could do with Judy's offering before I slammed the phone down.

I was and am a poor loser. I will never like people who aren't.

Ralph likely did some extra checking on me after that. A few days or weeks later he called me again and offered me a job at his shop, conditioning the offer on me getting off drinking and staying off it.

"I got a job for you, Al," he said seriously. "But only if you pry yourself off the bottle."

My first impulse, that day, was to tell him off, to say I could handle my liquor. It was a line I liked to use. But, that day, I saw my reflection frowning back at me in the mirror across from the phone. I saw what I was and how I looked. I had a sudden sane moment along with a realization of where I was going to end if I kept on my present course.

"I'll call you, Ralph," I managed to say. "I'll try to dry out. And thanks for thinking of me."

Ralph's call came on a Friday. The weekend that followed was the longest and hardest of my life. I stayed in my apartment and fought out a preliminary bout with alcohol, mourning the remains of my life, unimpressed with my assets.

I'd had promise, a present and a future. I'd made more money that I could spend sober. I'd had a beautiful wife, flawed, undoubtedly unfaithful, but lovely. I'd been treated with the respect that money and station in life can bring. I'd had a strong, efficient body and once had known how to keep it in shape.

Somewhere it had all unraveled. As a criminal lawyer I'd first tried to believe my job was an important cog in the machinery of justice. I'd defended my clients to the best of my ability even when I knew they were guilty. I'd played games with the courts and tampered with the justice system. Somehow that had fed my general malaise and become part of why I drank. I hadn't liked my job. There were endless numbers of ways to get defendants out of of jail and prison. There were hearings on top of hearings, dozens of motions and writs. There were arrays of courts, state and federal, overworked, stung with unaware and idiotic appellate decision that must be court-followed. I had a gift with books and words. Someplace, in the jungle of legal chicaneries, I could many times find an answer.

I'd fought early feelings of guilt. I'd told myself that the guilty were entitled to the best defenses their money could buy.

Judy's dislike of my practice was undisguised from the first. Her repugnance (and occasional fascination) with and for many of my clients had at first amused and later annoyed me.

Perhaps if the marriage had been good, perhaps if we'd worked at it, we might have stuck it out.

Criminal law was what I did. I was *the* criminal lawyer in my original office.

The marriage had come apart. For Judy there were others waiting in line, panting hard.

I stopped working out and began smoking for my nerves. My weight soared. My practice was hated and bothersome. I didn't want to represent scum anymore, but there was little else for me to do.

On the day Ralph called I was almost broke, suspended, fat, hacking my way through three packs a day, and not yet quite drunk enough to ignore the call.

I sat after I hung up the phone. I didn't have much left. Maybe a thousand could be raised through the sale of the VW Dasher and a few other remaining posessions.

I looked in my mirror and saw the bloodshot eyes and the unshaven, slack face of a loser. I examined my hands. Once they'd grasped the high bar and I'd swung around in exultant circles. Now they shook, were stained with nicotine, and could barely hold my ever-present cigarette.

I imagined myself wearing cast-off clothing, lying drunk and filthy in an alley, a grimy hand gripped around the neck of a wine bottle in a brown sack. Wine was the cheapest drink for an alcoholic and I was already a day wine drinker, liking it.

I didn't like my future vision.

I decided to try to make it *not* come out that way.

A friendly AA woman told me later that very few managed to do it the way I'd done it. Alcoholics needed help. After hearing her I resolved to go to AA if I needed future help, "a day at a time."

Quitting was hard and painful. It was fear and shakes and nightmares. It was eternally long days and endless, sleepless nights.

When the weekend was over I'd not had a single drop.

I'd walked a dozen restless miles each day.

On Monday I'd thought I might have made it, but Tuesday was bad and Wednesday not much better. Thursday I'd had the shakes. On Friday I ran a little and walked a lot.

I quit cigarettes that day.

It wasn't far from my place to Overton Park. I spent much of the crucial second weekend there, walking, jogging, resting between. I wanted cigarettes and something, anything alcoholic. I wanted a drink. To fight it I watched black kids play rough games. I tried to ignore the smell of open beer cans and the noises that blared from the suitcase-size radios many of the young carry with them as they wander this mean, but interesting world.

Sunday night, for the first time in nine days, I began to feel a little good. Now and then, when my heart wasn't racing, I'd get the old sense of well-being I remembered, the one that came after intense physical exertion. Now it followed a hard walk or a short jog. But it was there.

The better I felt the more I wanted booze. The first days I'd kept the urge stored away. On Monday of my first week I'd poured my small stock of cheap vodka and wine into the sink, leaning toward the smell. On Tuesday I wanted a drink so bad that I went out and bought a bottle of Popov Vodka and sat most of the day staring at it. I didn't open it, but I watched it (and it, in my imagination, watched me) that day and night. Wednesday I poured it out, crying all the time, but leaning away from the smell rather than toward it.

By Sunday Two I felt that if I ever drank again my life would end just as I tipped up my glass.

I swore to myself I'd never drink again. I looked into the future and knew that life was long and there were a lot of bottles out there in the haze of the coming years.

But I would try.

On Monday morning, ten days after Ralph's call, I dialed his number. My hands were reasonably steady. The yellow nicotine stains on my fingers seemed slightly faded. I had my private investigator's license in my lap, afraid I'd forget it and what I wanted to say.

Ralph answered the phone. His voice was cheerful. "Coin Shop."

"It's me, Ralph. Al Sears."

There was a moment of silence. I wondered if he was reconsidering. Then Ralph said, "How you making it, Al?"

"Better. I'm ten days without a drink. You mentioned something about a job. I could use one. Part-time or full-time?"

"Part-time now. Maybe full-time later."

I'd earlier recalled the layout of Ralph's Coin Shop. There ought to be room for me to put in a desk and a filing cabinet.

"Do you think you could rent me a little space and let me use your phone for local calls for part of my pay?"

"Doing what?"

"I've got a private investigator's license. I'd like to use it. Skip tracing, looking for witnesses. No rough stuff. No divorce work. No guns. No bandits."

He was silent again. "I guess that could work out. Maybe be good protection for my shop. Come past tomorrow morning about eight and we'll figure it out."

So we put it together. I worked for Ralph as needed. A few old clients and legal friends gave me occasional investigation work, mostly accident stuff, running down witnesses, plus a little skip tracing.

I lived.

I was where I wanted to be. I loved Memphis. It was a whoring Jezebel of a town by the dirty Mississippi River, population half black, half white. It was a mean and dangerous city, beautiful and deadly, a city where you worried about earthquakes and floods and getting murdered in your bed.

Now, out of my foggy past, maybe someone wanted to take away my refound life.

It couldn't be Ralph they'd put a contract on. He was one of the best men I'd ever known. I liked him a lot.

It almost had to be me.

There seemed little for me to do about it now. I needed to think and look. I needed to check my past. I needed to listen.

Outside my apartment window the last of the late-night swimmers had vanished while I mulled things. I rose, stretched and looked at my watch. I didn't run often in the wee hours, but I was too edgy for sleep. I thought a run in the night air might ease nerves.

I picked up my glass and took it into my tiny kitchen and poured out the off-color dregs. I washed the glass and placed it in the drainer before I went into the bedroom to change into running clothes.

3

Friday, July 19, 9:15 A.M.

FRIDAYS WERE USUALLY busy days in the coin shop and so I tried to reserve them for coins and not do anything for my other clients.

I could see Ralph watching me. In between customers, at a momentary lull, he said, "I was awake most of the damned night. The harder I tried to get to sleep the more positive I got that I'd seen that dead guy before here in the shop."

"How about maybe at a coin show?" I suggested. We did a coin show now and then, averaging perhaps one a month. There was, in fact, a big show coming up in Memphis in a week.

"Maybe," he said, considering it. "But I think it was right here."

"Maybe *you* did see him here, but I didn't. His face meant zilch to me."

Ralph shook his head, his eyes unsure. "Damn it all, I do remember him."

I waited.

"Did you see the morning paper?"

"No."

"We made the news. Not a big story. They had the right address and the story said something about that guy trying to rob

22

the place." Ralph looked down at a case of coins and then back up. "The only name mentioned was Harlan's."

I nodded. Ralph fell silent when business got brisk.

In the early afternoon, because Ralph kept asking me to at every break, I phoned Smitty at the PD.

"We found out his true name," Smitty said laconically. "It was John Shelton. They called him 'The Shell.' My guess is the nickname comes because no one ever managed to get anything out of him he didn't want loose. Two time loser. Heavy drug user. Intelligence on him says he had somewhere from ten to thirty contract kills. You were fortunate, Al. We didn't find any stolen cars near the coin shop so he either walked, bussed, or took a cab. He'd have had you drive him away in one of your cars. Cleaner for him that way. Someplace, sometime, we'll find his rental on the airport parking lot or somewhere like that."

"I see."

"Why was he interested in you or Ralph?"

"I can't figure it out, Smitty. If Ralph's got anything in his past then I know nothing about it. Maybe it's someone after me for something back the line. What bothers me is why did they wait this long? Hells bells, I wandered around drunk and readily available to a hired killer for a long time. I could have been erased then easily."

Smitty said, "That's sure seems right. But you keep thinkin' on it. If you or Ralph come up with anything then I want a quick call."

"Sure, Smitty."

I hung up and reported the conversation to Ralph. He shook his head and I could see he was still worried.

We closed the shop at five, but that wasn't the end of the day. Ralph had a newly purchased coin collection in the safe that we needed to mount in two-by-twos, code with cost, and then price. The collection had come from the estate of a wealthy Germantown man whose heirs now wanted their inheritance in negotiable form. So we pulled the coins out of the safe and looked them over again. Ralph did the big stuff, frowning as he reex-

23

amined each piece under magnification—tough date silver dollars, a 1799 ten-dollar gold Eagle in about uncirculated, and two sets of high-grade half dollars. I did the more numerous small items, proof and mint sets, some slider walking liberty and Barber halves plus the slabbed stuff. I still had a few pieces to go when he finished.

"Want a Whopper and some fries for supper?" he asked.

"Hold the cheese on mine," I said. I looked at the last of the purchases. The Germantown decedent had not had the best of eyes in buying the set. There wasn't a gem among the dimes and someone smart had already removed the tough 16D and the 21's before selling Ralph the set.

"And no fries," I called at Ralph's back. My stomach, after its years in an alcohol bath, rebelled at too much fried stuff. Today felt like that kind of day.

I had finished before Ralph returned. He carried his Burger King sack, an afternoon paper, and wore a look of excitement.

"Someone beat Benny Wilson to death downtown in an alley off Court Street," he said. "There's a story here in the *Press Scimitar*, plus another story about our robber." He shook his head. "It came to me, when I was reading the articles, that maybe I might have seen that guy when Benny brought him in here."

"Did you?"

"I think so. Maybe."

"Can you remember for sure?"

"Not for sure, but I think it was recently." Ralph tapped the paper. "The police said Benny was mugged. I guess they found him this morning."

I knew Benny. I knew him from lawyer days and from coin-collector days. He was a minor thief, a sometimes receiver of stolen property if he believed the stolen goods to be untraceable. He was a vest-pocket dealer, which meant he carried his limited stock in his pockets.

Ralph tapped the paper again nervously. "It says his wallet was missing."

I nodded. I wondered what had made Benny look prosperous enough to attract a mugger? Maybe the attacker had known Benny sometimes carried coins? And Court Street was Court Street, mean and dangerous.

Ralph handed me the paper. Both stories were short. Ours was a rehash.

Benny had died from several blows to the head and a crushed throat. It seemingly had happened, I figured from the news story, after the robbery attempt on Ralph's poker game and the death of The Shell.

So, no connection?

I'd bought a few coins from Benny, back when I was buying, and Ralph, I knew, had also bought from him down the years. In dealing with him it was buyer beware. Benny handled fakes, and Benny handled stolen stuff, but Benny also occasionally got onto good, unstolen coins, and he knew and loved coins. I remembered he'd been in the shop a few weeks back. I didn't remember him having anyone with him, but he could have had.

"Where'd Benny live?" I asked.

"Why?"

"I think I might go past there and see if I can find anything that might tie Benny to our robber."

Ralph nodded. "I guess I could find his address on a purchase slip somewhere."

"Dig it out. Benny died after our man was dead, but what with you thinking you saw the two of them together here I'll take a look where Benny lived."

"For fun or for marbles?" Ralph asked, smiling.

"Who knows. Someone invaded your poker game, knew us both, and maybe intended to kill us. I'd like to find out more. Benny getting his head beaten in might have a connection."

"It's police stuff."

"Sure it is, but the Memphis police are busy people. And, in the past, if I left my criminal defense business to the police without doing any investigation on my own I'd have lost some cases I didn't lose."

He looked me over and then nodded in assent. "I'm part of

it then. So maybe you'd take care of my interests for half price?"

I smiled and remembered Harlan's words. "Your friend Harlan said you were a skinflint, but half in this case is generous—especially when you could get me for free. It'll cost you a hundred a day and half the expenses."

"That much. Hmmmm." He thought about it for a moment. "You got it."

"Okay."

We grinned amiably at each other.

He went to the safe to find his purchase slips. While he did his looking I used the phone in my tiny office. I made five calls to the people who formed 90 percent of my business. I told them I'd not be available for a week or two and would get back in touch with them when I was available. No one got huffy. No one asked questions. I was sometimes useful, but easily replaceable. Or, on non-rush jobs, they could wait until I was free again.

Ralph found the address. We ate our sandwiches companionably, and then I went out into the hot early Memphis evening. I watched behind me carefully. No one followed.

THE ADDRESS RALPH had given me was in midtown Memphis, and that's now a peculiar place. For years it was a mixture of middle- and upper-middle-class residences, but then the retreat to the suburbs set in and the neighborhood declined except for a few isolated blocks that held onto their respectability despite hard times.

In the late sixties a few hardy souls decided to do what they could to reverse the retreat syndrome. They bought up old and oftentimes deserted residences, fixed them up, offered them for sale, and optimistically proclaimed the rebirth of midtown Memphis.

Commentators knew and publicly said there was no chance that it would come off, but to the surprise of the wise the renaissance began to catch on. Housing prices in the area began to turn upward for the first time in several decades. Midtown was still a far sight from being restored to its bourgeois greatness of the thirties, but it was moving.

I found Benny's place on one of the streets which had, so far, resisted renovation. There were no brightly painted houses in Benny's neighborhood, and no children playing. There were only rows of rundown, unpainted houses in varying stages of decay.

An old, bald man sat on his crumbling porch next to Benny's address snoozing in the last of the sun. He watched me and the street without real interest, maybe waiting for the night cool to come. He had his wine bottle beside him and I remembered.

I parked and got out.

Benny's address was a rambling two-story frame. The yard in front was overgrown with weeds. The porch swing hung at half mast on a screened-in porch where the screening gapped open in places like flaps of flesh around a jagged wound.

I could smell wild flowers, garbage, and green leaves, all mixed in with the germs of decay. There was half an hour of sun left.

Flies buzzed on the porch as I mounted rickety steps and crossed to the front door. I found only a cobwebby hole where once a doorbell had been. I rapped several times hard on the frame of the screen door and it bounced against the frame. Beyond the frame the warped front door stood open, exposing a dimly lit foyer, a long hall, and an ascending staircase.

I was about to knock again when I made out a shape moving toward me down the hallway. A voice asked disinterestedly, "What is it you want, mister?"

As it neared the door the form resolved itself into a large woman whose figure was draped in a shapeless housedress. She was of indeterminate age, somewhere between forty and seventy, and she could have been Benny's mother or his wife. Either way, chances were she'd respond to the name Wilson.

"Mrs. Wilson, my name's Allan Sears. I used to buy coins from Benny." I added a harmless lie. "We were friends."

"Benny got found dead off Court Street by the cops early this morning," she answered in a flat voice. She considered me for a few seconds and then turned away to retreat into the darkness down her hall.

"I know he's dead, Mrs. Wilson. That's why I came here."

She turned back and regarded me with suspicion. "You ain't no cop."

"That's sure right, ma'am. But I am a private detective. Have the police been here?"

"They sent two men. They came and told me what happened. One of them asked a lot of silly questions." She shook her head. "They didn't care much, but one of them did write down some of my answers."

"Maybe you'd let me look through Benny's room?"

She snorted disdainfully and started to turn away and terminate the conversation. I moved my hand toward my hip pocket and she stopped and waited. I fished through my wallet and came out with a twenty.

"I'm interested enough to pay," I said. "I'd like to look through his things."

"Only with me watching," she bargained firmly. When I nodded she opened the screen and let me in, deftly removing the bill from my hand as I passed her. I had a feeling that ten dollars would have done the job just as well.

She led me into a drab front room. There was a couch that made into a bed. There were a few faded chairs. The drapes were drawn tight again outside light. In one corner of the room there was an old pigeonhole desk.

"Benny did his coin things at that desk," she said.

I nodded thanks. I went to it. I sat in the hard chair in front of it and rummaged through the pigeonholes. There was nothing of interest. There were mounds of "Grey Sheets," which covered coin market prices by grade, handwritten lists of coins, and ads torn from the weekly coin papers. The drawers below were no better. They were jammed with old issues of coin magazines.

Something protruded from under the corner of a blotter on the desk. I lifted the blotter. There was a small folded piece of paper. I opened it. It was off-size, a scrap torn from a larger piece of paper. The scrap had some numbers scrawled on it. The paper had been wet once and the numbers had faded, but were still readable. The lowest number was 11, the highest 144.

There was another thing on the paper. It was a crude, hurried drawing of something. I turned it this way and that, looking at it from different angles. I was unsure what it intended to depict. It looked something like a design for a medal or a pin or maybe a coin design. It might also have been something off a whiskey label. I remembered that Benny drank Canadian whisky, V.O. and Canadian Club, sometimes lots at a sitting. A coat of arms like the ones on those bottles? Maybe he'd been drinking when he drew his design.

The woman watched over my shoulder. "What's that?" she asked.

"I'm not for certain, but it's the only thing I've found. Might I take it?"

She shrugged her permission, not caring. Her right hand was inside her pocket. I imagined it tightly clutching my/her twenty-dollar bill. Ten from me, ten from Ralph.

"Did the police say when Benny died? The time?"

"They said maybe three in the morning. That's what their docs told them."

"Did Benny play the numbers?"

"That's gambling, and so Benny did it. He gambled on anything and everying."

"Did he work any other place in the house?"

"No. He didn't work much here. Mostly he just slept here." She looked me over and loosened a little. "I'm his sister. Name's Bates, not Wilson now. His only sister. He didn't have no one else. And I don't have no one left now. When Ben wasn't sleeping or reading them coin things or a racing form he was there at that desk or, lots of times, out on the street." She thought for a moment. "Sometimes, when business or the horses were good, he'd give me a little money. All I got is a little left of Cyril's insurance and my social security. Ben wasn't no real problem. He never ate here. He drank, but not that much. Sometimes he'd come in late and I'd know he'd been into the Canadian because I'd hear him stumbling around and, later, snoring up a storm. He'd been doing a lot of that lately."

"Did anyone ever come to your house with him?"

"No. He did seem nervous-like the last few weeks, but when I asked him about it he'd grin and say it was nothin'. I'd see him watching close out the windows before he'd leave. Then he'd go out the back and through the alley, moving along quick for him." She thought on it and then added, "Once, a long time ago, the cops were after him. This time, if it was them, I never saw them."

I put the folded scrap of paper in my shirt pocket.

"How about phone calls?"

"It's my phone and in my name," she said. "He'd ask and use it now and then, but he never gave out my number, and I didn't allow no long-distance calling. My name's Bates," she told me again. "I was married and my Cyril died. He hated Ben, but I let Ben move in when Cyril was gone. Ben did most of his business in the streets and coin shops. He said he knew people watched him out there. He said it was bad and dangerous. But he'd said it for years. It was always silly talk to me—until now."

"Yes, not silly now," I said. "How about his stock—his coins?"

"I guess they was on him. The police said they didn't find nothin' and they ain't nothin' here. I looked good."

I nodded.

She smiled grudgingly at me. Something I'd said or done had made her decide a little in my favor. Part of it was, of course, the twenty dollars.

She let me open the couch-bed and poke under and into it. She let me go through each drawer in the desk again, this time piece by piece. There still was nothing. Ads and more ads, coin-show schedules, a poster for the next week Memphis Coin Show, a few copies of turf newspapers and magazines, some tout cards from Hot Springs, and a couple of horoscope magazines, maybe used to pick numbers or horses when all else failed.

"Sometimes he carried great big gold coins and wads of money," she said at her door.

"Did he ever tell you where anything came from?"

"No. He didn't say much. Ben was closemouthed. One day he'd be broke and trying to steal or borrow out of my purse. Next day there'd be money to spare."

"Was there a bank he did business with?"

She smiled at the idea. "No. No bank. His bank was on his hip."

I gave it up. "Thanks."

"You said you were his friend?" she asked curiously.

I felt compassion for her. The lie meant nothing. "Yes," I said, smiling. "Benny and I were friends."

She shook her head, wondering about it, but believing me.

At the door she said, "If you find Benny's coins . . ."

"If I find them they're yours," I said.

When I got to the VW, I could still see her watching me from her door, her face mostly lost in the sundown shadows.

I WENT TO my apartment and called Sue Whitten. She'd been my secretary at the firm where I'd first been associated. When I'd left them she'd stayed, wisely refusing my efforts to recruit her for more money.

We'd stayed friends of a sort. She was a wholesome lovely lady, ten years younger than I was, very bright and able. She'd been a top rate secretary. I'd teased her unmercifully when she'd been my girl Friday and bought her small presents and candy. Once, at an office Christmas party, I'd kissed her. There'd been a lot of kissing (and more) going on, and so I'd seized the opportunity and kissed Sue. The moment had wound up being more than either of us had tried to start, and it had kept things formal for us through the rest of the holidays and far into the new year.

I'd not called her for a long time. There'd been no need.

The phone rang twice and she answered.

I could hear soft music. "Yes?"

"Am I interrupting anything?" I asked.

"Allan?"

"I'm sorry to bother you, but I need to pick your brain a bit."

"Wait a moment," she said. In a bit the sound of the music died away. "All right. Pick away."

"Has anyone been around your office lately asking about me? Maybe some former client I represented? Someone I did work for in court? Or have there been any calls trying to locate me or obtain information on where I am?"

"Not that I know about, but it's possible. I'll ask around in the morning. Kate's still on the switchboard. She liked you and she still talks about you. She'd tell me—or you."

"Could you do it for me?" I asked. I didn't want to call the old office any more than was necessary. They'd let me go and they'd been right.

"Okay. Where do you want me to call after I find out?"

"I'll call you. Better, let me take you to dinner tomorrow night?"

She was silent.

"I'm both divorced and dry," I said.

"Are you Allan? Truly?"

"I am, truly," I said, not quite mocking her, but coming close. Now that I'd asked I found I wanted to take her to dinner. I remembered the Christmas kiss and the remembering felt good.

She was silent again. I suddenly felt like a young boy asking for a first date.

"Could I pick you up at your place about seven?"

"All right," she agreed. "Seven."

I hung up and thought about her some more. She'd come out of an Arkansas farm family to business college and from there to the law firm about the time I'd been named a junior partner. I'd rated my own secretary and I'd gotten her. She'd kept my files organized, my appointments straight, and my coat and pants buttoned. When she'd worked for me I'd made every single court appearance, even when I was hung over. She'd cajoled and bullied me into it. I sighed and realized what I'd let go. Not her, but the career. It was easy to feel sadness because of it. I'd flown high, gotten too near an alien sun, and had my wax melted.

But a few days back, in the lavatory at Ralph's, after cunningly finding and repossessing a hidden car, I'd found myself grinning in the mirror. I could now recite Grey Sheet prices line for line. I knew what to seek in grading coins. I could discern obvious fakes when they were attempted on me. And I was getting smarter at figuring the dodges used by skippers and hiders in my investigation business. All this had made some criminal lawyers, remembering what I'd once been, think about hiring me to track down reluctant, vanished witnesses. My business had picked up as time had passed. Word of mouth.

In the first days off alcohol I could sleep twenty hours, but now I was back to six or seven a night. My coordination was good again. When I reached out for something, I now caught it—things were where my eyes willed my hands to reach. I was almost thirty-five. I'd never again reach the physical condition I'd enjoyed as a youth, but I was close.

I thought about trying to track down Ace and Deuce to see what they were doing on this night. I considered shadowing Harlan or Duke. Do something. Instead I went home. I was still worn out from the night before.

I slept decently.

I CARRIED THE piece of paper I'd found under Benny's blotter to work the next morning, but I had to forego showing it to Ralph for a time. There were silver sellers. They appeared and disappeared with the rising and falling metal market tides. The price had risen sharply last week what with a new war threat jihad and jumped a dime again yesterday. With sellers, came buyers. The phone rang and Ralph answered, pricing bullion gold and silver coins. *For every action . . .*

I computed and made out receipts and wrote checks for Ralph to sign. Some places paid cash, but Ralph would not. If a buyer sold silver to Ralph he made a receipt for the purchase in the name on a furnished driver's license, and he issued his check to that name. The word on how he operated had spread. If there was stolen stuff around, and there had to be large chunks of it, we weren't getting it except from the boldest of burglars.

By noon it was quiet. We locked the door, pulled the blind, put up our BACK IN AN HOUR sign, and I went out for Arby's.

I brought back roast beefs and we divided them. I handed Ralph the paper I'd found at Benny's before I pushed his over.

"Look that over before gumming your Arby's," I said. "Tell me what you think it is?"

He gave it only a cursory glance. "It's a scrap of paper," he said acidly. "It's got some numbers on it, fifteen or twenty of them. There's also a drawing on the page. What else am I supposed to see on it?"

"I found it in Benny's room last night. What do you think the drawing is?"

He saw I was serious and examined the paper closely. "Probably just Benny doodling. It doesn't look like anything special to me, just numbers on a piece of paper."

"Did Benny ever sell in the numbers racket?"

"Not that I knew of. He'd bet on anything, but if you were running a scam of any kind, particularly a continuing one, would you let a guy as shifty as Benny be a salesman for you?"

"I guess not, but this he had hidden under his desk blotter. And his sister said he'd been edgy. No coins, no cash in the house. The police told his sister that they found nothing on him. Whoever got him picked him clean. And no bank box or hiding place in her house."

Ralph shrugged and handed the paper back. "They probably stole his coins when they mugged him. Means we got to watch out for Benny's fakes. Your paper could be anything, lockbox numbers, airline flights, numbers for Benny to bet on, lots in a subdivision, page numbers in a coin book or paper."

"It was all I found," I said softly.

"Eat up," Ralph said heartily. "You work the counter this afternoon. I want to make some calls and get the rest of this silver

34

out of here. We've got a show next weekend and we'll need money to buy."

"Sure." I could see he was excited about the show. It was the first big coin show in Memphis in several years, except for the annual paper-money show, which was mostly rag pickers looking for currency.

"I need to be out of here by six."

"We'll close before then. Got a heavy date?"

I thought about Sue and found myself smiling. "Not heavy, but not light either."

He patted me on the back after wiping his hands on a napkin. He liked it when I did normal things. We finished the rest of the Arby's and opened the doors again.

Before I left that night I took the paper I'd found at Benny's place, made a Xerox copy of it, and put the original in my file in the small backroom cubbyhole Ralph had given me for my private investigator working space. I put the copy in my wallet. In my PI room I had a table, a chair, one file cabinet, and an extension phone. Enough to call it my "office."

4

Saturday, July 20, 7:00 p.m.

At seven I knocked on her apartment door. She lived not far from my place in an apartment complex occupied mostly by bachelor girls. The windows of the apartments seen from the streets had plants and frilly curtains. Several crowd-bold, bikini-clad young ladies whistled at me as I skirted a sunny tennis-court/swimming-pool area. The whistles raised my spirits, although I suspected that anyone under the age of seventy might have drawn them.

She answered the door.

"Come inside for a moment," she said, examining me shyly. "I can make you a drink if you were just funning about not drinking when you called."

"No drink. I really have quit." I examined her in return. She was small and well formed. There were a few almost invisible freckles down her nose. Her hair was glossy brown, tightly curled in ringlets, a style I didn't remember on her. It looked good. She looked clean, bright, and completely delectable.

She took my hand in her small one and drew me inside and sat me on her couch. She perched on the other end of it, nervous as a mother bird at her nest, watching me.

"You don't have to take me to dinner," she said. "I found out what you wanted to know and I can tell you about that here and now."

"Maybe I asked you to dinner for more reasons than mere information," I said.

She blushed. I'd forgotten girls did that.

We proceeded out.

I took her to an ersatz Mexican place in the near neighborhood, she having expressed a fondness for that cuisine. She drank small sips from an enormous, icy margarita, and I drank pineapple juice.

"You look good," she said. "And you seem like your old self again, like you were when I first came to work in the office."

"Thank you. I'll take that as a compliment." I saw that she hesitated to drink her margarita when I was watching. "I don't mind seeing other people drink, Sue. It's only that I can't drink. Try thinking of it as if I had a bad cold and was on pills and under doctor's orders not to drink."

She reached out and touched my hand. "You hurt yourself so much, Allan. It was like you were a child's toy, wound too tightly, and had to be in motion every moment. Sometimes I thought you hated yourself and what you were doing, but you kept doing it over and over."

I took her hand in mine and cradled it. "I'd see you frowning at me. I thought it was funny at first. You were efficient enough for both of us. You were my official worrier. I thought I didn't need to worry as long as you were doing it for me. I guess, as things turned out, I did need to worry for myself."

She pulled her hand away gently. "What happened to your marriage, Allan?"

Thinking about Judy was no longer an onerous task.

"The same thing that happened to the rest of my life about then. It just went away like—like an alcohol rub. It evaporated."

"I saw Judy on the street the other day. She's back in Memphis working in television."

"I heard she was," I said carefully. There was more to it than that for me. I'd seen her at a distance once. I'd avoided contact, fled the scene.

"She's so gorgeous. She asked if I'd seen you."

Judy had been lovely, made for a winner, not a loser. But she'd had her own problems. I remembered the worst of them well and without fondness. *An old love, gone, hopefully forgotten.*

"Let's both of us forget Judy."

Sue nodded and sat back in her seat, becoming businesslike. She dug into her handbag and brought out a typed list.

"Some people have called about you over the past few months. There were several Kate didn't know who wouldn't leave names, but there were these other three whose voices she either recognized or who told her who they were." She handed me the small list.

I recognized one name immediately: Robbins Whitehead. I'd met him first as a dour, huge, disappointed suitor for Judy. He was her distant cousin, related to her in some mysterious and minor way going back to pre–Civil War days. He'd been around, under foot, and somewhat petulant, when I was hot dating Judy. He'd also been in evidence at the wedding, his doughy face polite enough, a man wearing his hair shirt visibly, but bravely. Judy had smiled at him then, been extra nice to him, taken him aside, and talked gently with him. He was, she'd explained to slightly jealous me, an old beau. I'd been gracious also, but I'd not liked him. *He was a loser then, and I was a winner.*

I wondered, with Judy now free, why he still had an interest in me.

The other two names sounded familiar, but I couldn't immediately remember why or where.

"Did you research them?" I asked.

She nodded. "I checked the office files mostly because I was curious. The one you obviously recognize, Robbins Whitehead, never was a client, but I've read and heard he's being seen with Judy and also being mentioned in the society columns with her. Nate Loveman, who wasn't in the office yet when you were there, but who's into old Memphis families, told me he'd heard on good authority they're supposed to get married."

I felt like laughing. "Judy's going to to marry Robbins Whitehead?"

"That's Nate's story. He keeps up on all the society stuff."

The possibility of that made things darken within me, but only for a moment. Maybe they were made for each other.

"How about the other two?"

"The other two are people, or relatives of people, you represented when you were in the office," Sue said.

I looked at the list again. Clement Johnson? Abraham Burks? Was it possible I'd represented them and now didn't remember?

"You represented Clement Johnson in a robbery case," Sue prompted. "You got it plea-bargained down to theft. He took a four-year sentence and did a short part of it. He got out of prison about six months back. I checked downtown with a girl I know in the prosecutor's office. She didn't know if Clement Johnson was in any trouble with the police now, but she did think she remembered the name from somewhere. She said she'd check and get back to me."

"And Abraham Burks?"

"Maybe you'll remember his wife. Mildred?"

I thought for a moment. "Mildred?"

She nodded and waited.

I did then remember a little. "Millie, not Mildred." Tall and tanned, a lot younger than her husband. Lots of money. She'd drank too many stingers one foggy Memphis night and then gone for a fast midnight drive in her Aston Martin. During the drive she'd smashed a pedestrian into bloody ruins and fled the scene. The dead man was a semianonymous bum walking the edge of the pavement on Riverside Drive. That had helped. The case against Millie, as put together by the prosecutor, hadn't been strong. I'd filed a speedy trial motion, forced a quick trial, ordered Millie to wear subdued clothes, and gotten her off by dealing her to a plea on an included offense, with a probated prison term, the bargain made and consummated on the day trial was set.

It seemed long ago, now. I remembered vaguely she'd made a few firm passes. It was during one of the waning periods of my marriage when I was drinking heavily. Perhaps I'd have taken her up on it if I physically could have, but all that happened were some furtive, drunken meetings outside the fences of her huge house and a few intense phone calls. My love had been the bottle. Millie had been fond of it also. She'd been one of my last clients with the firm before I'd moved on to single practice and solitary drinking.

"Do you remember her case?"

"Sure," I said. "Now I do."

"Her husband called. He was anxious to speak to you about a legal matter, according to Kate's almost infallible memory about what was said. She said he seemed distressed when he was informed you no longer practiced law."

I'd gotten the job done for her/them. I supposed I could cross them off my list. I remembered some more about the wife, Millie. I'd never taken her to bed, but I had sneaked out with her a few times, mostly on the pretence of going to coin shows. She'd been attracted to gold coins. Could it be that she'd misinformed her husband that there was more to our relationship than lawyer-client?

Something to check.

"What happened to make you call me after all this time?" Sue asked. "I got curious after you called about why you're checking now."

Slowly, trying to be matter-of-fact and not overemphasizing anything, I told her what had happened Thursday night. Her eyes got big when I described rolling the legs out from under the robber and feeling the heat from his shotgun blast. When I got past that point she reached out and took my hand. Some women, the good ones, think they can heal you by touching you. I didn't object to her hand in mine. When I finished the story she sat watching me, still holding my hand.

"Maybe it's not what you think," she said.

"I hope not, but I've got to check. Ralph gave me a part-time job in his coin shop and a place for an office where I can do a little private investigative work for extra money. I like both jobs. I don't want him hurt because he got associated with me. I'm almost sure it's me, not him, that this break-in bandit came after, assuming the armed burglary was a prelude to an execution. So I called you and I'm checking. I'll check out the names you gave me. Then I'll keep checking. Maybe a name I hear will lead me where I need to go."

"You were a good lawyer," she said. "Don't you want to do that again?"

"I'm not sure. I don't have to worry about it just now. The suspension still has more than two years to run."

She looked down at her plate. The coffee had grown tepid.

"Could you take me back to my apartment now?"

"Whenever you want. If you'd like an after-dinner drink first . . ."

"No. I have some pretty bottles of red and green liqueurs at my place if I decide I'd like another drink. So please take me home."

I paid the waitress. I led Sue to the VW. I watched around me, but there was nothing to see. No one waiting, watching me. The night was warm and I could smell the perfume in Sue's hair. She sat far away in the passenger seat, curled there. The nearness I'd felt between us earlier seemed gone.

But at her door she kissed me hungrily, took my hand, and drew me in the door after her. She whispered in my ear.

"I want you. I've wanted you forever. But you were never fair game."

An old feeling returned. When I'd been drinking heavily, I'd lost most of my desire and almost all of my ability. When I'd gone dry ability had slowly returned, but desire had remained elusive. Now, both were present.

I lifted her up gently and we made it into the bedroom. Once there, though, she changed her mind while I was in the midst of unzipping and unbuttoning.

"No," she said. "No." She pushed me away. "I do want you,

but not now or this way, Al. You frightened me when you talked about that man and his shotgun." She pulled her rumpled skirt straight and gave me a troubled smile. "Your Judy would still be in the way."

"Judy's gone for me," I said simply. "Believe that."

"Not if she decided otherwise," she said firmly.

I didn't think it would work that way. I'd had a pretty good dose of Judy. She was gorgeous, but we were divorced. I'd not contested that divorce and had, in fact, welcomed it. But that was then and now was now.

Sue could read indecision.

"Let's talk some more," she said. "I'll make us a pot of coffee."

"No more coffee, Sue. I'd like a real drink."

Her face changed.

"A real drink for me these days means a nasty Diet Pepsi or a go-to-hell big orange," I said lightly.

She brightened. She led me into her kitchen and poured me a diet cola. She sat me on one side of her kitchen table and sat herself on the other, trying to be businesslike again. She drank something she poured from a bottle she took from a cabinet. It was green and she poured it over cracked ice.

"Crème de menthe?" I asked, interested.

She nodded. I thought she was now making an effort to keep things between us as impersonal as possible. It was going to be difficult, because we were so close I could smell her hair and, with a quick, easy reach, touch her.

"I remember from long-gone days that I always thought it tasted like licorice strained through mentholated cigarettes."

She grinned and nodded. "That's an apt description." She lifted her glass and stared into it. "To change the subject away from things alcoholic, I want to tell you I went to your suspension hearing."

"Oh?" I asked. "Maybe you can tell me about it. I was there, but I remember very little of it. I don't, for example, remember seeing you. The hearing officer knew early that I was a drunk and a permanent drunk. He was a good man. I knew some in my practice. Ray Washam. Fine lawyer. Once, during the hearing, he took me aside and advised me to hospitalize myself and he'd delay the hearing for a time and maybe that would do me some eventual good. I refused. I don't recall what my situation was that day—whether I was drunk or just hung over. I guess I didn't think that a continuance would help. Everything had gone wrong and I wanted it all done with and over. If I'd gotten dried out then I'd have gone back to it. I didn't want to quit. Then."

"But you quit on your own," she said wonderingly.

"Sure. I quit because I finally decided I wanted to stop before spending my nights in the gutter, because something inside me changed. It wasn't easy. Now, I stay away from drinking because I'm scared of it." I held up a hand to forestall other questions about that bad time. "Tell me about the hearing. Why did you go?"

"I went because I was interested. It was a closed hearing, so I couldn't walk right in. I stood in the hall and listened because the door was never closed. There were some people there as witnesses I'd never seen before. There were some I had seen in the office." She shook her head. "I heard them talking and being questioned in the hall before they went inside. They seemed, as a group, mean spirited and vicious."

I nodded reasonably. "Lots of ex-clients tried to use my drinking to appeal criminal convictions. So they wanted me suspended or disbarred. But I heard the testimony and I wasn't set up, if that's what you mean. I screwed up things enough to get disbarred for life. Instead I got a suspension. The hearing and what came from it were more than fair to me."

"I still think you ought to take a long look at what happened in the hearing. Maybe someone who testified there wasn't happy when you got off with only a suspension."

I thought about that. "Could be, but it's unlikely. Most who testified got their chances to vent their spleens. I don't remember anyone seeming angry enough to kill me. But maybe I will take another look. The transcript should be available. At least I'll call Washam and see what he thinks."

"Having been the judge for the hearing, would he tell you anything?"

"I'd think so. He didn't want to hold the hearing. He got assigned the job by the state bar disciplinary people."

She shook her head, not understanding that part of my tricky profession.

I emptied my cold cola and smiled. "I'll go quietly out into the cold, cold night now. I will cry my way home. Thank you, Sue."

She nodded, not meeting my eyes, ignoring my bantering tone.

"You said something about Judy marrying again. Do you know when?"

"I'm not sure. I have the impression that it will be soon. Why do you ask? Are you going to question your Judy?"

"No. I've no interest in questioning her. She wouldn't tell me all the truth anyway, being incapable of so doing, and I wouldn't be able to distinguish between her truth and lies. Judy might kill, but only if you took a television job she wanted away from her. One more question for you, Sue. When she gets married can I come back to see you again?"

"Yes," she said softly.

"Thanks for that," I said. "It'll keep me warm for a while."

She took the few steps with me to the door. Once there she put up her face for a kiss.

"Stay with me," she said, still uncertain about it. She looked away from me, then sighed and took my hand, and led me back.

But in the night Judy was there in our midst for her, if not for me.

I left the apartment just after midnight, creeping out quietly. I was almost sure she heard me dressing, but she lay quietly.

I WAS IN the "Cat's Cradle" Bar and Grille by one in the morning. The bartender in there was an old acquaintance, if not a friend. Once we'd lushed a lot together. He'd had his drinking partially under control then and I hadn't had mine under any kind of halter. Now I was in control and he was still where he'd been before, a man who drank too much too often, and was tortured by it.

His name was Eugene "Gene" Foxmyer. He was about my age, burly large, a man who looked and sometimes acted pugnacious. He liked wearing good clothes. He'd flunked out of law school and failed in business. So he was a bartender.

I picked "Cat's Cradle" because I knew that some of the Memphis cops hung out there. I also picked it because when Gene and I were hanging together we'd also hung some with Duke Theotokopolis. The Cradle had been one of our favorite watering holes.

At one in the morning the inside of the bar smelled like cooked onions and old spilled beer. I drew in an appreciative breath and proceeded to the long bar. At the far end of it two men argued something about basketball loudly. Both were drunk, but still friendly. Gene stood near them, watching and waiting. He was a suspicious man and a born pessimist. He'd bartended here and there all over Memphis, good at it, but not trusted because he drank too much.

He saw me sit down and frowned over at me. He tapped on the bar to make sure he had my attention.

"Cola or diet cola?" he asked contemptuously.

"Make it diet. I need to lose a few pounds yet off a very fat head. Get yourself a drink on me."

He brightened, but only a little. The owner of the bar had put in metered drink dispensers recently and I'd heard around that those had become a problem for Gene. No more free drunks by shorting customers and saving shots for his own consumption.

He meter poured a scotch for himself and hand poured a diet cola for me and brought them.

"Does Smitty come in here much?"

"Police detective Smitty?"

"That's the one."

"No. Maybe one or twice a year. Those black cops got places they go of their own. Get free drinks, maybe free women."

"Seen Duke?"

He shook his head and sipped his drink carefully. I could see he'd had a few, but he was okay. "He doesn't come around here that much these days. I hear he's got tax troubles, I hear he's got law problems. I hear that lots of people are hard watching him and that some of them would like to catch him. Last time he was in here he talked about moving to Europe, Switzerland, or maybe Greece."

"How long ago was that?"

"A week, maybe two weeks. No longer. He said he came in here looking for you, like he thought maybe you were into drinking again. Did you fall off the wagon anytime recently, Al?"

"Not yet," I said.

"Well, he was in here looking for you and he bought me a couple of drinks." He smiled a tiny smile and looked down at his glass. "Just like you should if you want me to tell you a tiny thing additional."

"Help yourself to another on me," I said.

He got another and added a little ice. "He had that blonde gal with him. Your ex-wife."

"Judy?"

"The one works on television. Pretty girl. She came in with him when he was looking for you."

I found that slightly startling. One of my clients Judy had professed hating was Duke Theotokopolis. Once he'd come to our apartment and postured for her, playing his game of being covert aristocracy. She'd laughed at him then and never had a good word for him afterward. She'd said, many times, that he was a "Greek greaseball."

I wondered, without there being much jealously to it, what she'd been doing with Duke. *Other than what came naturally.*

"And they came in and said they were looking for me?" I asked.

"That's what they said, but I'm not sure they meant it, Al old son. They went out of here after a couple of drinks. They were acting by then like they were very old and dear friends." He smiled maliciously at me. "I bet that ain't the first gal you've had that Duke stole. We got a waitress works evenings who thinks he's prettier than a bulldog pup."

"Who was paying for the drinks?" I asked. Sometimes, if Judy was after a story, she bought.

"I don't remember. They'd been drinking for a while and were hanging on pretty good. I don't know who had the wallet, but I'd guess it was old Duker."

"Was it a Friday or Saturday night?" Judy didn't work Saturday or Sunday and Friday and Saturday nights had been her time to let down her hair and panty hose.

"I swear I'm not for sure. Maybe."

I wondered what Judy and Duke had been doing in the bar. I picked some more, but Gene had no further ideas, and so I let it go. I listened to him on politics, war, and the Memphis scene for a time. I finished my Coke, checked my watch, and went home.

My dreams were of Sue, but Judy was there also, a tall, nude figure in the background, set to watch and wait and get even for all the money I'd blown down the drain in the drinking spree before our divorce.

I awoke once and figured it would take her a while.

5

Sunday, July 21, 4:30 A.M.

THE PHONE REAWAKENED me. I'd come home from talking to
bartender Gene, taken a run in the park, done some exercises, and
gone to bed. The feeling that someone was watching me had remained, but if there were watchers I couldn't pick them out on
the street or from my window.

The caller was my once-client Duke Theotokopolis. "I need
to talk to you, Al."

"Gene call you?" I asked.

"Why would he?"

"I heard around you'd been looking for me before the poker
game. Okay. Talk away."

"Not on the phone. I've no faith in either my security or Ma
Bell's these days. Sometimes I think old governmental friends
are still watching me and could have my phones tapped."

"You know I don't practice law anymore, Duke. And I know
you don't collect coins. So I can't advise you in the legal area. I
work for Ralph and I do a few simple things as a private investigator. I skip trace and I repo cars."

"I don't want advice from you, but you may want mine. I want
to tell you some things that could save your life. Let's say it's something like Brutus should have said to old Caesar, or Hastings

48

should have told the Tower princes. I mean you and I are friends and you've helped me lots in the past. Now maybe I can help you."

"That sounds interesting. Where and when?"

"My suite. You remember where it is?"

"I remember, if it's the same place."

"It is. I don't like moving. You come. We'll talk."

Duke lived up high in a plush apartment building. I'd been there before, but it had been a while. The last time I'd been there for a party I'd sampled a lot of what he kept in his liquor cabinet. The good stuff. And I'd seen the contempt in his eyes for me as a practicing, perpetual drunk before my own eyes went completely vacant. I'd awakened on his couch and had to have two or three Bloody Marys before I could make it home.

I drove there and found parking. A doorman called up to check to see if I really was supposed to go inside. The doorman had seen me before, but it was that kind of building.

Duke met me at his door. He was carrying a drink. "Mine's a screwdriver. You used to like them and it's almost breakfast time. Can I get you one or something else? You may need it."

"No. Nothing for now." I looked at his glass. It was massive, cut-glass, with small rampant lions around the gold-plated rim. I remembered he liked those.

"All right, if you're sure. I'll finish this and we'll have a little walk outdoors." He swished it around, perhaps trying to tempt me. I shook my head. Social drinkers, who know you've once been a drunk, will sometimes try to tempt you back into the arena of the bottle. It's easy for them to stop and so it should be easy for you. *Maybe it's something in the genes?*

He led me inside. A huge window opened onto a railed area with a view of one of the city's nicest residential sections below it. I'd admired the view before at night and in the daytime. Duke lived first-class. Living good had been one of his problems with the unbelievers at the IRS. They'd looked at his returns and his way of life and gotten suspicious.

The room was furnished with swank, decorator-picked furniture. Crossed swords and medieval shields decorated dark wood

49

walls. There were two bedrooms opening off the central room, plus a dining room, a huge kitchen, and three baths. I'd never seen the place empty, as it was on this early morning. When I'd visited before there'd been girls and drinks in abundance. I wondered if he'd brought Judy here and found I didn't give much of a damn.

He drained his drink. "Sure we can't have one together?"

"No, thanks."

He set his glass down regretfully. "Too bad you never learned to use this stuff in moderation." He made it sound like a character flaw within me. "Ah well, come on, and let's walk."

I followed him to the elevator. Below, the doorman opened the big front door for us, smiling at me now, bowing to big-tipper Duke.

"I got treachery stuff to tell you," Duke said, when we were away from the building. "It's hot enough that I didn't even want to do it upstairs. If they got my phones bugged, then maybe they also got something hidden in the apartment. I get the place swept now and then by experts, but how about the times in between? The word you need to know is that bad dudes are still after you."

"No stuff? I'd never have thought it," I answered, barely concealing open sarcasm. "What I need to know is what it's about? What's going on? And who's paying for it?"

"I'm not sure. All I found out is that someone big and mean is out after you. I heard it a couple of places." He shook his head. "Maybe it's just follow-up because of what went down at Ralph's last Thursday—a ripple—cause and effect."

"Who told you?"

He shook his head. "The one who told me said I wasn't to say where I heard it. He meant it, Al. He said I could tell you, but not give out his name. He's big, but he acted scared. If I gave you his name you'd know it. I think you did some things for him one time."

That could be just about anyone.

"How about telling me the place where you heard it?"

"Just a bar, Al." Duke looked me over thoughtfully. "If I was you I'd take me a long vacation away from Memphis. You need money then I'll loan you some."

"That's generous of you, but what good would a vacation do? If someone really wants me they'd either find me or wait until I got back."

"Maybe things would cool down given time. Or you could take a permanent vacation. Ralph, he's got friends in coin places in other towns. And I got some friends in New York who could use a smart guy like you. You could be of service to them there. They'd like you just fine."

I walked along. I looked around. The people on the street all seemed to be watching me. A car passed slowly. I realized I was edgy. I'd already assumed that the fact that the contract killer had died wouldn't lift the contract.

If I left, I might take the heat off Ralph, maybe yes, maybe no. I didn't like thinking that someone was looking for me, watching me. I'd always been a noncombatant, a legal advisor. Now, for some reason, I was the game.

"I'll make you a deal," Duke said, looking sideways at me, his face intent. "You go in and rescue what I've got in that lockbox. You take it and hide it for us someplace else that's safe. Then you watch and wait. No one comes you give me two thirds of what's in the box. I'll give you the lockbox key and you can learn the signature the box is under. I can maybe try and make sure there's no bank problems." He shook his head. "They can't still be watching. Can they?"

"Maybe they are, maybe they're not," I said. "But I'm not interested."

"You'd make three or four hundred thousand dollars," he said. "How in hell can you not be interested. Here you are working a dollar-a-day job and driving doggy wheels that look about to fall off."

"Did you get me over here to warn me that someone was after me or to try to rescue your lockbox?"

"Both, but mainly to warn you. I thought maybe you might know or realize that someone wants you dead, but I wasn't sure.

If you run you'll need dough and the lockbox is the closest I've got to it right now. How about half and half?"

I shook my head. The money in the safe-deposit box had been skimmed off a junk business that Duke controlled. I'd set up the corporation for him. He'd issued the stock to what I suspected were graveyard inhabitants. On paper Duke owned nothing. In actuality he owned all. The junk business wasn't that good, but he'd run stolen cars through the twenty-four-hour junkyard, removed the usable parts, then crushed what was left. More money had been made from that part of the operation than he wanted to show on his taxes. So he'd put a major part of the skim in a long-term lockbox under a bogus name. It was still there. Next year, if my memory was right, the rental on the lockbox would run out and that could cause problems unless Duke found some way to either empty the box or pay continuing box rent. I thought he was bright enough to figure a way.

I thought also that he'd forgotten or was ignoring the fact that I already knew what name the box was in. In my old files, now secreted in Ralph's basement, there was a copy of the signature card. Or maybe he remembered and wanted my reaction. I wasn't going to rescue the lockbox cache for him or for me. I'd had big money before and it hadn't meant much to me. All I wanted to find out now was who was after me.

"Not me, Duke. You want what's still in my files I'll give it to you free gratis. You've got a lot of contacts. Try someone else."

For a moment his eyes sparked, because he didn't like to be denied. Then he shrugged and smiled. He prided himself on being smooth. The name "Duke" had come because of his Greek immigrant father's affection for John "Duke" Wayne, but it meant something more than that to Duke. He'd taken the name seriously and carried it steps further. He had great affection for books about ancient Egypt and Rome. He was versed on the monarchies of Europe and Asia. He believed, I thought, in a natural aristocracy and considered himself to be a part of it.

"It was a thought," he said philosophically. "I think sometimes about all that money getting mossy there. I thought of it this time partly because of you and your problem. Believe that, please."

"Sure." Easy to say.

"I'll try to find out more about the problem," he added brusquely.

"I'd appreciate it. One more thing. Gene said you were in his bar with Judy looking for me. What was that about?"

"She called. She was looking for you. She thought maybe you'd be at Gene's and she didn't want to go in there alone."

"I have a phone number of my own. Why not try me there? And you knew I was working at the coin shop."

He smiled. "She wanted to look for you at Gene's." He nodded once. "If a girl looking like Judy called you and wanted to look for me someplace would you argue?"

His logic seemed unassailable.

We parted company near his apartment building. I found the VW and sat for a moment in the front seat before starting it, considering Duke. He was bright, inventive, and a continual plotter against the rules. He had no real love for me, despite what he'd said. I'd been useful to him. Maybe he hoped that, one day, I would be again. I doubted that he had much affection for anyone. But it could be he'd warned me because he owed me an old debt. *Nah.*

I shook my head, started the car, and drove back to my place. The sun was coming up when I got back. I went inside and caught some sleep and later, a small breakfast.

I was up again and out in the VW before noon.

The streets of any large-size city can be confusing if you're not a native or a longtime resident. Memphis is no exception. Union and Poplar are two of the major east-west traffic arteries in downtown and midtown Memphis. Poplar continues on eastward through the suburbs, a mixture of black and white, through Germantown, and on out to Collierville. Union's course is shorter. Just past Airways it dies in name, part of it splicing into Poplar and the other dropping under Poplar and then heading slightly north of east under a new name—Walnut Grove.

At the point where Union/Walnut Grove has its identity crisis, some minor commercial establishments and a couple of large warehouses line a little-used street beneath the elevated roadway. The largest of the warehouses must once have served a more conventional purpose, but now, on Saturdays and Sundays, it was a permanent flea market. There on any weekend you could buy junk jewelry, comic books, political pins, used clothes, antiques, and ten thousand other things, including coins. I'd been there. Once I'd picked up a 1901 Bison note for about a third of what it was worth, but much of the stuff was overpriced.

Getting there was easy enough for me because I knew where I was going, but a stranger might have driven around all day without finding the warehouse. Today I wasn't looking for something cheap to buy. I went because Ace and Deuce went there. It was the only place where they had a constant table. Most of their buying was for their auction list, and most of their selling was from that list. The list had a post-office box return address. The telephone number on their cheap cards was a restaurant they frequented.

I found them both at their table. I nodded at them and looked to see what they had in their ramshackle display cases. A stream of people went around me. There were no lights mounted at their table to see by, but the huge room was reasonably light from overhead skylights.

"I think you guys purposely don't mount lights so your buyers can't see how bad this stuff is," I said, nodding at the cases.

Ace grinned. Duke watched me carefully.

"What do you hear?" I asked.

Both of them shook their heads.

"Nothin', Al. And there ain't nothin' around this place today either," Deuce said. "You know if there was good stuff we'd have already snarfed it up." He smiled. "Did Ralph ask you to come and look us over or tell us somethin'?"

"No. I'm on my own, looking, but I guess you could say I'm looking for Ralph and me. I keep hearing around since Thursday night that someone hates my guts bad enough to want me dead. I just wondered if you guys had maybe heard anything like that?"

and me that some of the robbers are saying what they were to do in the show was steal the gold and steal the cash. Leave the rest. They'd then have melted the gold down and sold it in bulk. Untraceable and five or ten million maybe. Maybe another million in cash. A Duke's deal. The biggest of his life. He worried about me tieing it to him. So he set out to kill me, kill Benny, and maybe he'd already killed one other."

"You mean Millie?" Sue asked.

"Yes. Like I said it's something to check. There's a place she used to meet me when she'd sneak out of Abe's. It's not there anymore, but I could maybe find where it once was. It used to be on the edge of Abe's fence. I remember vaguely that there was a lot of underbrush and small trees. I used to walk in back there." I nodded at Harlan. "It could be worth Smitty's time to check that area. Maybe Duke met Millie, charmed her, talked her into getting her gold coins, and then killed her after she came through the fence and buried her around her hidey-hole, but off of Abe's property. He had to get the money from someplace to front the robbery, buy the guns and dynamite and the truck. If Smitty isn't interested the word could leak to Abe."

Harlan smiled. "If Abe ever decides Duke killed Millie then theres no way in hell, in prison or out, that Duke will live a month." He looked at me. "Do you care?"

"No, but I won't personally tell Abe. My bet is he'll find it out on his own. He may already know it. He's a bright man. Was he here tonight?"

"No. He called and declined. Very politely. He said he'd like to talk to you one day," Harlan said.

I thought some more. "You've got to understand Duke. He's a man who plans. He will and can wait for good things. But he can't stand being a loser. He automatically knew Benny would fink on him, and that I'd tell Ralph. He'd eventually lose the biggest deal of his life. And, assuming he did get Millie's coins then she'd be another matter that had to be neatened. So he started to clean up things ahead of time. I found out, for example, that he was in a bar with my ex-wife Judy. Supposedly they were looking for me. All friendly and all. If I died he'd have Judy to say that all he'd ever had for me were the fondest of feelings."

"How about his feelings for Judy?" Sue asked acidly.

I smiled. "I guess they were fond also. But Judy can do that to most men."

"I know one she'd best not try it on if she wants to have any future at all," Sue said.

"When did you become dead sure it was Duke?" Ralph asked.

"I was dumb. I was never sure until the night Sandman and Micko poured the booze through a tube into my stomach. Not until then." I smiled at Harlan. "Up to that night I was pretty sure it was you."

Harlan grinned. Sue and Mary Roberts exchanged smiles. It was all a joke now.

"It's just difficult for me to believe an ex-cop is an honest man," I said semiseriously.

"You'd better believe from now on," Harlan said. "And how about how I feel? You're a damned ex-lawyer. I've no use for the legal breed."

We nodded at each other comfortably.

"Under certain circumstances Duke could come up with the money to pay a big-buck lawyer and maybe make bond," I said, thinking of that.

Harlan shook his head. "I believe you're talking about a stash he made a long time ago. In a lockbox? I will tell you that it's probably not there anymore."

"Who did that?"

"I heard it was neatened a long time ago by a couple of tax men who retired. The federals that are left on the case still think it's there and Duke still thinks it's there. I believe it isn't. And I promise, cross my heart, I had nothing to do with the taking of it."

I shook my head. "That's funny because that stash was likely the biggest reason that Duke wanted me dead. He knew I had the name it was in and a copy of the lockbox card. I could, because he knew I needed the money, steal what was in the box. Or, if his robbing Ralph made me angry, have turned him in on the lockbox."

"Gone," Harlan said.

"One more thing," Ralph said. "I was to do this about the time we were all ready to get out of this place and go home to bed. I'm ready." He handed me a tiny package. "Open that," he ordered.

I had difficulties because of the right arm still in its cast, but I managed. Inside the paper there was a plastic holder. It held the 1802 half cent that had caught my eye at the opening of the coin show.

"Some of the boys thought you ought to have this. I suggested the chain cent, but so far this is all they'd pop for. It's a gift from them to you."

I examined the coin in the poor light. It was a handsome trinket. I put it in my shirt pocket.

"You tell them all thanks a lot," I said. "And thanks to you for saving my life by giving me a job, Ralph." I smiled and looked at Sue. *I'd wait for a while and sell the half cent.*

Then, I'd use the money and buy something for Sue.

If I was going into collecting she was going to be my chief collectible.

For keeps.

Both now watched me. Ace was the first of the pair to nod.

"I might have heard a little," he said. "I can't remember where it come from." He leaned forward. "I just heard it said around, after the story in the papers, that maybe that night at the game might not be the last time someone would try to get you. I guess it's for something bad you did. Bar talk and coin talk is that someone wants you in the grave."

"And of course you hurried right over to me to tell me about it?"

He smiled.

"Who's saying it? And is Ralph involved?"

"It ain't Ralph. If it was him then I'd listen better so as to tell him. We owe Ralph." He nodded at me cryptically. "I don't know you real well and I don't care about you to more than tell you the rumor now that you asked." His look said: I'd not cross the street to help you.

"You know only this rumor you say you heard?"

"Right. People we see whisper that the guy who broke into our poker game didn't care about Ralph except for some quick coin dollars. Just you, Al."

"I hear there was maybe a someone who was in our poker game who got to Benny that same night. Were you guys buying stuff from Benny?"

Deuce smiled virtuously. "You had to watch Benny too close for us to mess with him much."

Ace nodded pious agreement.

"Bullshit. You guys were his best customers and now he's dead." I pulled out my billfold and got out the scrap of paper with the numbers. "Either of you ever seen this before? Or do either of you know anything about the numbers written on it?"

"Not me," Ace said, looking away, not wanting any part of my document.

"Nor me," Deuce echoed. He squinted at the paper, but his face showed nothing.

"You guys know an Abraham Burks or a Clement Johnson?"

They exchanged glances that were irritated. "Question time's over, Al," Ace said. "We don't know nothin' that can help you and we ain't going to do no checking for you. Do your looking else-where. It could be bad for us to be seen talking to you. A man never knows who's watching."

I eyed them, frustrated. They "liked" Ralph, but not enough not to steal from him. He'd told me they'd switched coins on him at least twice and that lately he'd suspected them of stealing small stuff when they were in the shop. I'd been told not to turn my back on them and to show them one coin at a time. They didn't like that or me, but Ralph smiled and let me do the showing to them while he sat in the background or talked on the phone. I was the bad guy to them, Ralph the peacemaker who invited them to a poker game when he could find no one better to fill a seat. I knew they'd bought many things from Benny, because I'd seen lots of things Benny had tried to sell to Ralph on their auc-tion lists.

Ace and Deuce were small-time players in the coin game. There was a fabled time, in the sixties and seventies, when any-one could make money in coins. But now the market was full of knowledgeable buyers. Those buyers wanted papers showing things were genuine, they wanted grading, they wanted prove-nances—where did this coin come from? And yet Ace and Deuce had to make some money from somewhere. They ate, they slept, they put gas in their Crown Vic.

"I'll give you a rumor to spread," I said. "Tell it around that you guys were messing with Benny and now Benny's dead and people are wondering why."

"Benny got mugged is all," Deuce said. "We're not your pals. We owe you nothing. Leave us alone. Move on. You're blocking our cases. What we do here is part of our living. It ain't like we could go back to practicing bandit law again until the next time we got suspended." He smiled tightly. "It ain't like we were hot-shot private eyes."

I wanted to jerk him from his side of the table to my side, but that would do no good. Ace read my eyes and moved back a step.

I said in a soft voice, "Either or both of you had best not try fooling with me or stealing again from Ralph. Business isn't good business when the buyers are thieves."

They eyed me with naked hate in their eyes. I was saying openly what had remained unsaid before. Things would never be the same again for them with me.

I wasn't sorry.

I moved on. I sat outside the old warehouse in my car for a time. I waited and watched. Ace and Deuce knew my car, and so I'd have to follow from a long way back.

I waited. Eventually they came out of the flea market carrying two junk display cases and their coins in a suitcase. I watched them load.

I stayed behind them, almost sure of where they were going. They lived about a mile from the flea market in a tiny apartment. Across the street was the run-down restaurant whose phone they often used and where they ate most of their meals. They took the suitcase with the coins inside with them. I waited and waited some more. I sweated in the car, got out for the breeze, and sweated some more outside.

When Ace and Deuce came out of the restaurant they still had the suitcase. They looked around, checking the neighborhood. I was a block away, standing in the shadow of a building. I was pretty sure they'd not seen me.

They carried the suitcase with them across to their apartment.

When it began to get dark I went back to my car. I watched from there until it was full dark. I gave it up when the last of the lights in their apartment went off and neither of them came out of the building.

I moved on.

6

Sunday, July 21, 9:45 P.M.

I GOT BACK to my apartment and did another needful thing. I uncapped a diet cola and then called Ray Washam, the lawyer who'd held my hearing when I was suspended. The phone rang ten times without anyone answering. It was Sunday night. Maybe he was gone for the weekend.

I tried once again that night before I went to bed. There was still no answer.

Trial out of town? Vacation?

I read some and then slept.

In my dreams someone offered to sell me a box of faked coins, 1944D pennies made to look like the rare 1914D's, silver dollars with etched mintmarks, and a roll of 1916D Mercury dimes. The coin crooks were smarter than I was, so I bought the coins and wound up finding out later. In the dream there was always a drink near my right hand, and, regrettably, I was drinking what was there as fast as I could, glass by glass, while I constantly smoked cigarettes.

I awoke in a sweat. I listened. In the night there is always someone inside your place, someone waiting to do you in bloodily. The feeling was so strong that I got up, moved around inside the apartment until I was sure I was alone, and then went to my window. Outside, where I could see the street, there was nothing. But then something moved in the darkness and I saw a man walking. He seemed to be looking up in my direction and so I stepped away from in front of the window. When I went back to it the man was gone.

I slept some more, this time fitfully, waking, then dozing. *Why in hell would someone want to kill me at this stage of my life?*

I FOUND ROBBINS Whitehead easily on Monday morning. He was "in" stocks and bonds, suitable employment for an "old Memphis family" aristocrat. Robbins was that, multi-money. He was, for his profession, part of a brokerage firm in the 100 North Main Building. I took a long lunch hour with blessings from Ralph the boss. I wore the best of my old summer suits, a conservative blue tailored by two gentlemen named Mr. Hickey and Mr. Freeman. Now that I'd lost booze weight the suit fit well again.

I took an elevator about halfway up the building. The halls smelled of medicine, cleaning powders, bug sprays, and duplicating machines. Whitehead's firm's door had a host of names on it and an invitation to walk in. I did so.

"I'd like to see Mr. Whitehead," I told the pretty, dark-eyed receptionist.

She gave me a look that approved of Mr. Hickey and Mr. Freeman and buzzed Whitehead.

"He'll be along in a moment," she promised.

"I hear he's about to marry," I said conversationally.

She smiled, apparently having heard that, too. "It's that television girl. He's crazy about her."

We both fell silent, thinking our varying thoughts about that.

In a short time Robbins did appear. He looked a little different than he'd appeared at our wedding, surely larger, but not a lot heavier. He was a big man, four or five inches taller and maybe sixty or seventy pounds heavier than me. He had a sullen look to him and was building a pot belly, although I knew he was not yet thirty-five. There were dark bags under his eyes and his jowls drooped. A drinker. *Takes one to know one.*

He saw me and did a double take. "Al!" he cried, as if delighted to see me. "I've been trying and trying to find where you vanished to. What's happened to you? I tried to run you down through your old firm, but no one there knew exactly what you were doing." He glanced coolly at the receptionist, who was watching us with interest. "Follow me back to my office, please."

I winked at the secretary and walked obediently behind him. I thought he was both surprised and nonplussed at seeing me.

"You look good," he said heartily, once we were inside his office cubicle. "I heard around that you'd stopped drinking." He patted an ample stomach. "I truly need to do the same thing. Perhaps I'll manage after Judy and I get married. Right now I'm having to wear my old Hart Schaffner and Marx corporate model work clothes and can't get into any of my good things."

"You and Judy are getting married?" I asked, feigning surprise.

"Sure. Hadn't you heard? The wedding's in a few weeks. We made the decision months ago, after things didn't work out as she wanted them in Chicago and she came back here. That's why I tried to find you. I wanted to tell you up front, man to man."

"I see."

"I certainly hope this doesn't wound you too much," he said smiling, but only a little. "I've loved Judy all my life. It broke my heart when you temporarily stole her from me." He gave me a good-old-boy grin. "Both of us know Judy. She needs a little time to settle down and adjust to the right life. I can give her that kind of life." He turned away and glanced out his window as if thinking about that. Then he turned back. "Have you seen her since she came back to Memphis from Chicago?"

"Only once."

"She hadn't told me that," he said, alarm in his voice.

"I doubt she saw me. I saw her at a distance, Rob."

"I see," he said, liking the sound of that. His voice took on a touch of command. "I hope it remains that way. I know she was badly bruised when the two of you broke things up. It was an unfortunate experience for her. Perhaps it was that for you also. But women suffer much more than we men do in such situations."

I refrained from laughing. "Yes," I said politely, willing to acknowledge whatever blame there was for the failed marriage.

He held out a pudgy, patrician hand bearing a signet ring. I took the hand and shook it tentatively. Despite the fat it was a strong hand. I remembered Judy had told me he'd been a shot putter at Harvard.

"Now that she's mine I'll see she's never hurt again," he said confidently. He then gave me a careful look. "And I know you'll help, Al."

"I wish both of you nothing but the best," I said.

"Thanks," he answered heartily. "Your saying that means a lot to me. I always liked you." He looked pointedly down at his watch. "I'll tell Judy you were by to see me. And now I'm afraid I'm running late for a luncheon appointment."

"With Judy?" I asked.

"This one is, regrettably, business. I have my job and Judy still has her little television thing. I guess it'll remain that way for a while." He shook his head, perhaps not liking the idea of sharing sweet Judy with anyone or anything.

I shrugged and got up with him. I followed him down the hall. The receptionist had vanished into the noontime witching hour. I separated from him at the elevator. He went up and I went down.

I got back in the VW and found myself with ambivalent feelings. I found it hard to believe that Judy would marry Robbins Whitehead. He was below her style by a dozen miles. I believed our divorce hadn't hurt Judy; I doubted that anything like that would ever hurt her. She'd wanted me when I was a semifamous athlete and a member of a good law firm. I was something she was proud of owning. But, though she'd owned me, I'd never owned her. She'd operated her own life. A few times during our marriage, even early on, I'd been fairly certain she'd crawled into someone else's bed as part of whatever station intrigues she had going. Some late nights had to be explainable only that way.

Once, when things had been fairly open and shut, I'd accused her, but she'd sat and let me rant for a while, then denied all.

Such beliefs hadn't helped our relationship. But I didn't blame her for my problems. I'd made troubles for myself. She was one of those troubles, but not the cause of my difficulties.

Alcohol.

If she'd done a little genteel and covert bed hopping when we were married, I wondered how long faithfulness to Robbins Whitehead would last. Gene, the bartender, had already told me she'd been around with Duke. My guess became that Judy would joyfully accept Robbins for his big family house with its pool and tennis courts. She'd dress him well for parties with the famous and near-famous she knew, and use his family wealth and connections as a launching pad for her daily activities. For that, if he was good, she might let him into her bed now and then.

I also decided, if the chance came, she'd cheerfully give him up to try life up the television ladder again. She'd once told me, in a fit of honesty, that she had dreams of standing on the lawn of the White House doing an exclusive interview with a youngish president. Inside her golden good looks there was a mind/heart that calculated all and coldly planned. By now she'd determined, rightly or wrongly, what had gone wrong in her first foray into the Chicago wilderness far north of Memphis. My bet was she'd already done a lot of planning to avoid new mistakes.

Yet, in a way, I was mildly jealous. Something which had once been *sort of* mine was going to be *sort of* someone else's.

I thought about the merry chase she was sure to lead Robbins Whitehead and found myself smiling. I didn't like him. He'd patronized me before and done it again today. I'd let it happen because there was nothing else to do. Now I believed he was, late or soon, about to wear more horns that all of Santa's reindeer.

Along with the smile was the nostalgia. Once, for a time, I'd loved Judy. It was hard to rid myself of the inner feeling that I still did love her.

Youthful dreams.

I was no longer a young boy dressed up in a letter sweater and wearing my old fraternity pin and Judy was no longer my dream girl.

AT THE COIN shop that afternoon business was slack. I had some time to go through the phone book and check a name Sue had given me. The book listed a whole raft of Johnsons, but no Clement Johnson. I then called Sue at my old office and had her give me the address we'd had on him from his retired file. That address was on Winchester, which meant he was mostly likely black. I tried to remember exactly who he'd been, but things from those times were too foggy.

I also got Sue to dig into Millie Burks's old file. There was a phone number listed in it, and, better, an address. I remembered the address vaguely and thought I could find it again. A couple of times I'd picked up Millie Burks near it.

Sue's voice on the phone was businesslike.

"I thought I should leave early to ensure your reputation with your neighbors."

"Yes," she said. "I woke up and you were gone."

"I found out today that Judy is getting remarried in a few weeks. If you aren't sure I'm untied from her now, could you maybe believe it then?"

"I'd try very hard," she said, voice grown softer. "I really must go now."

"Can I call you tomorrow?"

She waited a long moment. "You can call me when you want."

"How about I take you to dinner tomorrow?"

"No."

"Yes."

She was silent. "You come to my place about six and we'll talk about dinner."

"I'll be there."

"You'd better be. I'm a jealous woman."

63

"I hope so. And thanks also for the information."

When I'd rehung the phone joyously I went back to the directory. I went through the long lists of Johnsons twice, but no Johnson was listed at the address Sue had provided. I tried hard again to remember anything about Clement Johnson as I sat fingering the phone directory. A little came back to me. If I remembered him at all he'd been young, black, a first-time adult offender, but with an extensive juvenile record. I thought I also remembered they'd caught him firmly, maybe inside a place and in the very act of committing burglary.

He didn't sound likely as a candidate.

Abraham Burks wasn't listed in the directory either, but I recalled he was big money and figured he had an unlisted phone number. I dialed the one Sue had provided and got an interrupt signal. A recorded voice informed me the number I'd called was no longer in service. I then tried information, but the cool voice that answered had no new number for either a Clement Johnson or an Abraham or Mildred Burks.

I decided to drive out to the address I had been provided for Abraham Burks.

We closed down at five. Ralph went upstairs. I followed him up, carrying some of the good pieces. During the week, after business hours, he'd take some coins up at nights to study and admire. He loved coins. Being a coin dealer was a perfect life for him.

"You finding out anything?" he asked. "And do you need any money?"

"No to both questions. Some people came in looking for me after I left my old office. The only one I've been able to run down so far is a man who was and is heavily interested in my ex-wife. He might kill for Judy, but not just yet." I smiled, thinking about that and thinking about Judy being out catting around with Duke Theotokopolis and cheating a little on her intended. "I don't think he feels threatened. He may in the future."

Ralph smiled at my smile. He knew a little about Judy. *Enough.*

"One thing you need to know. I had a run in yesterday with

Ace and Deuce at the flea market." I recounted what had happened.

Ralph laughed wryly. "It was bound to happen sooner or later. They're likely only petty thieves," he said. "Maybe afraid to steal much."

"Or maybe not. They could have set the poker game up by telling this Shell what was going on and where."

"Far fetched," he said. "But I guess it's worth a check."

"Maybe they do know something worth knowing about another person out there looking for us or me, but I doubt it."

"I could maybe go around where they are and talk nice and see if they'll say anything?" he asked.

"Whatever," I said, not caring. I didn't think, in retrospect, that either of the two knew anything that would help me/us, but I wasn't dead sure.

"I'll do it if it works out that I can," he said. He smiled a small smile. "I kind of like the idea of them being mad enough to stay out of the shop. Maybe it'll save a couple of thousand a year."

"I hoped you'd be tolerant."

"I saw you earlier riffling the phone book back in your private detective corner," he said, sitting down carefully in his favorite chair.

"I found nothing. I do have an address to check out, though. I'm going to do that now. Write this down." I gave him the address. "If I don't come back tomorrow, have the Memphis police start checking from that spot." I looked around his apartment. He had deadbolts, one high, one low, on every door. The windows were barred and they were high off the street. If the door had been bolted we'd never have been visited by the dead intruder and, now, it would take a determined thief and an unwatchful Ralph for a someone to gain entrance.

"Stay back away from the windows," I said.

He fretted in his chair. "I feel like I'm in jail. There's a movie I'd like to see at the Plaza. A Stallone."

"Let me do what I need to do and then I'll come back fast if it's early enough. We'll both go."

"How come it's safe out for you and me, but not for me alone?" he asked. "And you don't carry a gun and I do."

"One reason is the last time I took in a movie with you I heard you snoring before it was halfway through. I, at least, will be awake."

"I'll still take a gun along to the movies," he said, grinning now. "I got me a carry permit."

I shrugged.

Sometimes he was like a small boy getting ready for a Saturday cowboy movie. Me telling him I'd return later for a trip to the movies had brightened him and given him something to look forward to.

He was a man with great knowledge of his field. He knew coins and paper money like no other dealer I'd ever known. Outside that, his vision was limited. Cards, action movies, Colonel Sanders chicken, Big Macs, Whoppers and fries . . .

"I'll be back," I said. "Bolt the doors."

"Sure, Al. You're the boss in this project. But I get worried thinking of you out there checking on bad things."

"Me, too," I admitted. "You shake and I'll shiver."

7

Monday, July 22, 7:35 P.M.

THE ADDRESS SUE gave me for Abraham Burks and wife was far out in Germantown. I headed the VW up Highland and turned east on Poplar. The evening weather was lovely and I rolled down the driver's side window to smell the mixed aromas of flowers and hydrocarbons.

It was a long way out to Germantown. I found the house easily enough, once I got close, because I did remember it. It was huge, Georgian in style. It sat far back from the road on a small knoll. The property was surrounded by a high chain-link fence. Signs every fifty feet or so pointed out that the fence was electrified at times. There were rings of barbed wire at the top of the fence with bayonet-like protusions attached to the wires. Along the inside perimeter, as I drove by, a large man walked a Doberman pinscher. My recollection now was that it hadn't been that secure when I'd been representing/seeing Millie Burks. But I was unsure. Drink enough alcohol and it damages you. Heavy drinking cuts subtle little chunks out of your memory and leaves you with the scarred remnants.

There was no guard at the gate, but it was closed and locked. A phone was in the gate wall. I lifted it.

There was nothing for a time, but I remained patient. Then a male voice asked, "Yeah?"

"My name's Al Sears. I once represented Mrs. Burks in a legal matter. Mr. Burks was trying to reach me some time back. I'd like to talk with him if that's possible."

"What about?"

"Probably about why he was trying to reach me."

"Wait," the voice ordered tersely.

I waited.

The voice came back on. "The gate will open. Drive inside. Stop and wait just inside until the gate closes. Make sure no one enters with you or behind you. We assume you're alone?"

"I am."

"All right. Drive up and park your car in the circular drive in front of the house. You'll be met there. Others will be watching the gate and the drive. You be sure no one follows you inside."

I did as I was told. No one followed behind me. I waited until the big gate closed behind me and then drove up the asphalt drive and parked in front of the big house. I got out and stood by my car, waiting patiently.

A man came outside. He watched around for a moment and then nodded at me. He went to my car and inspected inside it.

He was a youngish man, younger than me, athletic looking, very strong. He was also extra large. He moved quickly and well. I noted he had what appeared to be a gun bulge underneath his tan jacket.

"Keys?" he ordered. I gave him my keys. He opened the trunk and looked in it. He bent down and observed the underneath of the VW. When he was satisfied he smiled a cool, meaningless smile at me.

"Mr. Burks is waiting to see you. He told me to tell you that you're a most welcome guest."

"Sure seems that way."

He frowned. "Don't be foolish and take offense at necessary precautions. Mr. Burks is an important man. You undoubtedly know that."

"I'll try to bow correctly," I said.

He gave up on me and turned away abruptly. I followed him into a wide entrance hall done mostly in mirrors that reflected us. The carpet was thick. There were dim lights in the ceiling. He led me back through a huge room with windows all along its outer side. Beyond the glass there was an Olympic-size swimming pool. I tried to remember if I'd ever been inside before or if I'd picked up Millie and discussed business with her/him at my office. I remembered the outside of the house, but not the interior.

I wasn't sure.

Abe Burks got up from a chaise lounge. I thought he was maybe sixty years old, a small, dapper man. He wore a tiny mustache above a bright, silk dressing robe. He smiled and shook my hand enthusiastically. "My Lord, it is Al Sears. I tried hard to find you a while back. I almost went so far as to hire people to do the finding. Now the mountain comes to old Mohammed."

He led me to a chair. The big guard disappeared, but I had the feeling he wasn't far away.

"This place has more security than a bank," I said.

"Some nasty folk don't like me. That's one of the reasons I tried to find you, Al. It's not the main one."

"I got suspended from law practice, Mr. Burks. I still am suspended. Before that happened I went out on my own, left the firm, and was in practice by myself for a short while before they suspended me. Now I'm not drinking. I'm a private investigator and I work at times in a coin shop in the city."

"I found out some of that. It's why I quit looking for you. I didn't figure you'd know anything about what I was trying to find out."

"What was that?"

"About Millie. She disappeared a little less than two months ago. One day she was here, the next morning she wasn't. For a while we had cops all over this place. They dug up the gardens, they brought their search dogs inside the grounds. They even had teams out muddying up my private lake with drag lines." He pointed his finger out the window. "They didn't find anything and neither have I. I looked for you hoping you might know something. She doted on you." He held up a hand. "I know you didn't do anything wrong with her, although I'm sure, knowing Millie, that she tried. I had to keep a close watch on her. Millie was impetuous. Now and then I had to discipline her. Sometimes I also had to discipline one of her male or female friends, but I know you treated her nice and as like a lady as she'd let you. Not only that, but you saved her from a prison term."

"The most I remember about it is taking her to some coin shows after the trial."

"And maybe a little more than that," he said smiling, but only a little.

"That was when I was drinking," I admitted. "So, it could be."

He nodded sagely. "You were into drinking all right. Millie became very interested in gold coins. You could always count on her to get into expensive stuff. Sables and Jaguars and, for a while, until they soured, Aston Martins. She kept going to coin shows on her own after losing interest in you. She bought some things. When she left here the gold coins left with her."

"She's gone and her gold coins are also gone? At the same time?"

"Yeah. Best we can tell she got them out of the upstairs safe the night she left. I'd not known she had the combination, but she did. She took nothing else but her coins. I had her grounded, but she got out some way. The fact that she did get outside the fence and thereafter disappeared with her gold has made me more cautious. We beefed up the watch inside the fence." He shook his head. "I know deep down she's got to be dead by now, Al. I've got a lot of contacts and they've watched for her. But there's nothing. And Millie never could live in a vacuum. She wasn't that kind of lady."

"No one contacted you about her?"

"Not ever. I thought, for a time, that someone had her and I would get a call and a demand, but there was nothing."

"How did the police get into it?"

"I made a mistake. I called them. A couple of guys came out

here from the sheriff's office. Pretty soon there was dozens of cops crawling all over this property. They had search warrants, cold faces, and most of them wanted to put me behind bars on suspicion."

"What exactly is it you do that got them so excited, Mr. Burks?"

"I'm into a lot of things. I own some real estate. I got some stocks and bonds. I have a little piece of some action in Atlantic City and a smaller piece of Vegas. I'm semiretired, but there are people who still call on me for advice when things need settling. I invest money for some of friends of mine who use my services."

"Are these people who use you Mafia?"

For a moment I thought he was going to get angry, but then he stolidly shook his head. "The Mafia's a bunch of cavemen, Al. Yokels. They're into a few good things, but no one trusts them with much. Too violent. I'm not part and have never been part of that. Most of my big-money interests these days are in Texas and Florida."

Drugs maybe? I decided not to say the word. It seemed very out of place in these plush surroundings and to this small, dapper man.

"And so Millie and the gold coins disappeared and you looked for me?"

"Only after the cops quit digging for her. I think they finally decided I got rid of her in the river or somewhere, but I didn't." His eyes fell from mine. "She was great for me. She was shallow and vain. She could spend a day making up and putting on clothes. She was elemental. Now and then she'd try to hot trot someone else to bed, but I lived with that and got over it." He sat down on the edge of a chaise lounge. "Someday I'll find out what happened. I've still got some people looking."

"It could have something to do with me," I said softly.

He eyed me carefully like I was a new bug for his collection. I felt a cold, small wind blow over me. I hurried on. I told him what had happened at the fatal poker game. I told him about dead Benny. By the time I was done he was interested.

"I'll pass on to my people what you've told me. The guy who raided your poker game may be known to some of my people. To my best knowledge we never used him, but I knew a little about him and his reputation. 'The Shell.' A quiet man. Useful, but never to me or mine."

"Did he ever work for anyone in Memphis that you know about?"

"Once, years back. A political deal." He thought for a moment and then shook his head. "All those people are dead or in prison. Were you ever in politics, Al?"

"No. And I tried hard to avoid political causes in my practice. Being politically inept kept old and young judges from getting angry at me."

"It's not politics then. Like I said all them people are dead now except two or three who are still in prison. Maybe Shell saw you guys when he was in town before on the political thing, like maybe three or four years back. Or maybe he heard about your Ralph, checked out the coin shop, and decided to do an independent robbery."

"He knew me," I said.

He smiled at me. "Shell would use care and look things over before he came calling. The world is full of evil bastards, Al. And maybe Shell knew your name from hearing it in the coin shop or a bar or somewhere."

"Maybe." *Ralph had thought maybe Shell had come into the shop with Benny.*

Burks waited, still at my disposal.

"Do you know anything about the others at the poker game?" I'd supplied their names when I'd given him the story on the attempted robbery.

"I know something about them all. I know Ralph a little because Millie liked him. They say he's square. I know Ace and Deuce bought coins for Millie. I guess they cheated her some, but not enough to get me angry. They knew she came from this house. I know Duke, but he runs his own show. He never worked for me and I'd never hire him. Odd dude. Pompous and arrogant."

"How about Harlan?"

"I'd look hard into him if I were you. He's got a lot of irons in a lot of fires. I'd never trust a retired cop who suddenly makes a lot of dollars."

"How about the gold coins? Is there a list of the ones Millie took when she vanished?"

"Sure. I'll have Lefty make you a Xerox copy."

I waited for it. I shook hands gingerly with Abe Burks and with Lefty. I followed their directions about how I was to exit the gate.

I DROVE CAREFULLY back to Memphis, thinking about what Burks had told me. No one seemed to be following me.

I collected Ralph and we took in a movie, lots of action, lots of blood. Stallone against the world. An even battle. Stallone won.

Afterward we got drive-by pizza and took it back to his place. He put his huge gun under a couch pillow and drank cold beer, while I had a diet caffeine-free cola.

I told him about Abraham Burks.

"Why would he live hereabouts?" he asked. "I mean in Memphis?"

I shrugged. "I don't know. Do you remember him being in the store with his wife? She was a tall lady, tan and handsome. I never saw her in there, but she disappeared only two months ago. She bought foreign gold. Money would have been no problem. And Burks says he knows you."

"Let me see your list."

I handed it to him and he looked it over.

"I remember those folks. The reason you didn't see them is they'd call for an appointment and come after hours. I sold her some coins on this list."

"Have any coins you sold her turned up for resale?"

73

"Not that I've seen." He thought for a moment. "You sell something and you remember it, Al. Comes back it's like a child returning home. If any I sold her ever come back into the shop I'd likely know them."

"Sure, I know that. Abe says he thinks she's dead. Could I talk you into getting hold of Harlan Roberts tomorrow and seeing what he can add?" I smiled. "With the warning to you that Burks doesn't trust Harlan."

"Okay. I'll call Harlan and talk to him, but for a better reason than seeing if he wants to tell us anything. I trust him, Al. I think you should also. When that guy was trying to shoot his shotgun it was Harlan took him off your back. If that bandit had gotten two bangs at you with his shotgun you might not be here."

"I agree with that. What's your better reason?"

"I think I've got something coming that he wants. A piece of currency. National, third charter five. A state he doesn't have." He sipped his beer. "I think it should come in the mail tomorrow. Arizona, and Arizona notes are tough outside of Tucson and Phoenix. I got him a Holbrook." He looked out his dark window into the night. "I'll ask him generally what he knows and I will mention Abraham and Millie Burks's names, but no more than that. I will be very gentle. I trust him."

"Sure," I answered soothingly. *He could trust Harlan, but I wasn't ready to do that. I remembered a man I'd defended who'd shot a house burglar he'd hired to kill his wife. When things went down wrong he killed the burglar. Everyone thought he was a hero until they started checking the burglar's bank account and my client's checkbook.*

I waited and watched Ralph lock up. I walked to my car alertly, ready to run. Running was probably my best defense to an attack. It was, at least, something I could do to protect myself.

LATE THAT NIGHT, after thinking about it, I started the business of contacting Willie Farr. I did it by calling the telephone numbers of three places I knew he frequented and leaving my name and number at each place. No one admitted knowing him, but each place took my name and telephone number.

The three places I called were all gay bars.

Willie Farr called very late. I'd given up on the late-late movie and gone to bed. I came out of sleep instantly when the phone rang.

"Hey, Al, baby. What's shaking? It's been a real long time. I got your message."

"I could need some help, Willie."

If there was hesitation it was only a fraction of a second. He owed me and knew it. Three or four years back he'd been tried for murder and I'd defended him.

"Whatever you want," he said simply. "Is it money?"

"No money. No guns. Someone tried to kill the coin dealer I work for and me last weekend at a small-time poker game. Maybe you read about it in the paper. Then someone did kill a man named Benny Wilson, who my boss and I know well. Benny was a petty thief who was into coins. Same night."

"I never read newspapers." He was silent for a moment and then continued, "I mean, they're full of death, wars, and bad business news."

"You still in the gun business?" I asked. I knew that once you could have bought anything from Willie up to an antitank gun.

"I never discuss things like that on the telephone," he answered. "I used to have a smart lawyer who told me not to do it."

"Your lawyer was right. Could we get together sometime tomorrow? I need to talk to you about the things that have happened. And I need to ask you questions about people, particularly a man named Abraham Burks. You know him?"

"I know him. I know 'most everyone. I also know a bit about your problems, but not from any newspaper. I've heard it said for certain it was you that the Shell was after and not your coin shop owner. Shell died so I didn't call. I figured it was over."

"Maybe yes, maybe no. Tell me what else you know?"

"Not on the phone," he said. He was silent for a moment. "Your place or mine?"

"Your choice."

"Come to mine, then. Red gets worried when I go out and he can't see everything that's happening. If you come here then he can pray over us."

I knew Red a little and I smiled. "Thanks, Willie."

We set a time and I hung up.

Willie Farr was a black homosexual and he was a friend of mine. He was also one of the toughest men I'd ever known. In the melee that had led to me defending him on a murder charge he'd admittedly killed two white men with his knife in a street fight. One of those two men had shot and wounded Willie in the course of the fight. Willie had taken the stand in the trial and testified the two men had attacked him, which the prosecution had disputed. I'd found a witness to the fight, a witness who was reluctant to testify at first. I'd kept that witness under whatever cover I could under the rules of evidentiary disclosure. I'd placed his name on a four-page list of witnesses, a list too long for busy prosecutors to check closely. When I'd called my surprise witness the state had found a lot of trouble. The jury had been out less than an hour. *Not guilty.*

Willie had been grateful then and he still was. He hadn't kissed my feet, but he'd said, and I'd believed him, "If you ever need anything, Al, then you call me." He'd pushed a hard finger against my chest. "Hear?"

I'd heard. I'd not called before.

Willie knew lots of what went on in Memphis. He knew a few of the top blacks and a lot more of the bottom blacks in the city. And, being Willie, I knew that he'd tell me only what I needed to know.

I sat thinking about Ralph. I was certain now it was me the dead robber had been after, but was I certain enough to tell Ralph that? The week had aged him. I could relieve his mind by telling him he wasn't a target, but there seemed still to be a slim chance I was wrong in my preliminary suppositions. An unwary Ralph could be a dead Ralph. Now, in the coin shop, I'd noticed he kept a gun close to him at all times. When the door opened he'd always look up, his eyes wary until he recognized the customer. If a stranger entered he'd let me handle him while he sat watching carefully, gun nearby. At the movies he'd been relaxed fully for the first time since the robber had come through his unbolted door.

I looked at a clock. It was now after one in the morning, but I knew Ralph would still be up. He'd be perched in front of his TV, feet up on a hassock, an opened beer beside him, watching a late-late something with blood to it.

I called him and he answered on the first ring. I told him what Willie Farr had told me. I didn't take him out of it, but the conclusion was there if he wanted to grasp it.

"I don't know," he said, when I was finished. "All this stuff sounds real crazy to a fat, old coin dealer. I'm sitting here watching TV and I worry about me and I worry about you. So I'll stay with you. Like you said, half the normal fee, half the expenses."

"Thank you." I remembered something else. "Thursday night is setup for the big coin show. We need to start planning for that. Lots of your old pals will be in town. You'll get to see people you normally don't see. Quit worrying, but stay watchful. At least through the coin show."

"Yeah," he said with enthusiasm. Memphis was having the annual show for the Mid-American Numismatic Association, one of half a dozen "big" shows around the country in summer. That show was one of hundreds of shows annually, shows that ran from one day and a dozen dealers in a tiny hired hall, to huge shows like the ANA (American Numismatic Association) with five hundred dealers, lasting a week.

MANA was someplace near the top. It was larger than most state shows, a big regional three-day coin circus. They were expecting 160 dealers at the Kaleidescope Hotel near the river. Ralph had a table. I think he'd rented it more for the social stuff, the camaraderie, than for the show itself. We'd pack our stuff in and set up Thursday night, and the show would last three days, being fairly frantic on Friday and Saturday, then dying off in the afternoon on Sunday.

"I'll get to see some new stuff at the show," Ralph said, his voice light. "There could be two or three hundred million dollars worth of stuff on the floor."

I remembered my own lost collection with minor regret. "Yeah."

"You'll help me set up Thursday night for dealer's bourse?"

"Sure. No problem."

"Great. No public inside, just us hotshot dealers trying to cherry pick each other. I've got a want list. Maybe I can pick up some of the stuff on it."

"You sound excited."

"I am. I've not been to a big show for a while. You get hungry for a one. Not excluding the annual paper money show, this is the best one to come to Memphis for a long time. And this one won't be all rag pickers, like Harlan's damned Memphis paper money show."

"I thought you liked paper money?"

"Only because it weighs less than coins."

We hung up. I thought about going out and prowling a little more, but decided against it for this night.

I went to bed.

8

Tuesday, July 23, 4:10 P.M.

TUESDAY AFTERNOON, WHEN things got to slack time in the coin shop, I drove to Willie Farr's. Willie lived in downtown Memphis, in an old building that had recently been gutted and reclaimed into luxury apartments as part of the downtown renaissance. I couldn't see the appeal of living cheek and jowl with insurance companies, department stores, and various corporate headquarters, but lots of others did, and they'd spent large sums of money for the privilege.

I found a parking spot after cruising awhile and then walked a block plus to Willie's building. At his door I pushed a button and faintly heard a chime play a weird melody inside.

I remembered that the inside of Willie's apartment was always like a hothouse. Willie liked it warm. Sometimes in the winter, when even Memphis gets cold, Willie flew down to Grand Cayman and spent time there. But in summer he just stayed in his apartment, windows down, air conditioner off, liking it at ninety degrees, loving it at a hundred.

Red answered the door. He was white. I knew him a little. When I'd defended Willie on the double murder he'd been around, constantly wringing his hands, worrying about Willie, and worrying openly about my defense of him. Having won I then became one of his heroes.

He leaned out the door. "I do love that breeze," he said archly. "Willie wants you to come in. You'd be smart if you took off your clothes."

Willie had quickly become adjusted to the fact that I wasn't and never would be a switch-hitter. Red still had hopes of conversion. He'd told me, at the posttrial victory party, that I was "hot looking."

I grinned now and shook my head. "I'll sweat, Red."

I followed Red on back. We walked through a dim, stifling living room and a lighter, hotter dining area. That opened onto a glass-jalousied porch. Willie sat there in baronial splendor surrounded by his plants. He was almost ebony in color. He wore an afro and not much else. There were a hundred plus plants. They stood in pots on the floor, they hung from the ceiling, they crowded each other on the walls. Tropical plants, rich and green. The air was acidly sweet from their smell.

Willie was reading a thick book. He was a bright man and he'd made, in my times around him, some canny observations about the world and its problems.

"Here's Al," Red announced.

Willie nodded me toward another seat. Red stayed near the door, watching us. I wasn't sure whether it was jealously or curiosity.

"Go fix us something to drink," Willie ordered gently. "Coffee for me. What would you like, Al?"

"Some kind of diet cola."

"We got plenty of strong stuff. Anything you want?" I saw he was watching me.

"I haven't had anything alcoholic to drink in a while, Willie."

He smiled, pleased. "I'd heard that. I guess maybe you drank up this life's quota already, eh Al?"

"That's as good a way as any to put it."

He nodded, still pleased. "I've been asking some questions for you. I asked in places where I can ask. I heard some about what happened at your card game. And I heard about Benny Wilson. No one will say for sure why there's someone after you and no one knows why Benny got hit. He didn't pay off a couple of years back, but that was supposed to be cool, or at least they're all saying it was. And the guy who was trying to do you at Ralph's place, they say he cost lots of dollars." He shook his head, marvelling. "How'd you take him? From what I heard he was supposed to be the best."

"He thought I was too scared to do anything. I was almost that scared."

"You're tricky and smart, Al. I knew that when I hired you. Most of the men I deal with, plus Red, would have liked it better if I'd hired one of the city butter-and-egg black lawyers who do a lot of business in court, but when you got me off that made it all okay." He grinned whitely at me showing strong, even teeth. "No one ever got anyone off the way you did it for me."

I nodded. I'd gotten a break when I'd started checking the fight in which Willie had admittedly killed his two *victims*. I'd hung posters on neighborhood telephone poles. I'd persistently asked questions in an area where it wasn't deemed too bright to ask them. And Willie had made up part of the difference. Even though he was a homosexual Willie was an integral part of his neighborhood. The two who'd come in after him had been white thugs, interlopers. The neighborhood was 99 percent black. Soon I'd gotten me a witness to the fight. He'd seen my posters and checked me out. He was white. He told me later that for a white man to live in the neighborhood and do any good, that man needed to live silent. But on Willie, he'd asked around, the neighborhood had approved, and so he'd contacted me.

I'd first met with him, after his call, as he played basketball in a high-fenced lot behind a Catholic school. He was dressed in Levis, a too-bright shirt, and his was the only white face in a game with tall black boys not much younger than he was.

I'd asked, "Did you see the start of the fight?"

"I saw most of it. I ran into a bar and used the phone to call the police." He smiled. "That's frowned on here. I've spent a lot of time and effort to get them to trust me in the neighborhood. So I didn't say anything or admit the call when the police came. I watched like the others." He nodded at me. "They kind of like the little black dude in the neighborhood. They say he's gay, but still they like him. So I can testify for him. And he didn't start it. He did finish it. The others had guns. He didn't. With the facts being the way they are why is getting it dismissed such a problem?"

"He sells guns for part of his living. The police don't like him and have been after him for a long time. The two gentlemen who assaulted him were angry because he'd furnished some guns uptown where they didn't want them furnished, where they'd warned Willie not to furnish them."

"So I just testify to what I saw? I hope you understand I'll tell the truth? Your Willie did knife them. He moved quick with that big knife, faster than them. He got shot, but he still knifed them."

"That's okay to say just like you said it. You tell the jury about the guns and exactly what you saw. You get asked if I told you to say something then you answer that all I told you was to tell the exact truth. I got a prosecutor who thinks he can get big time for Willie Farr. I'm hoping you'll help a jury say no to that."

He nodded.

When I presented him to testify at the trial, he wore slacks and a T-shirt. I'd called and asked him to appear that way. In my direct examination I was purposely vague about who he was. All I asked him was his name and address, then I led him through the eyewitness stuff. He came across good.

The young deputy prosecutor eyed him cynically and went after him hard on cross, trying to make it look as if he was bought and paid for.

"You say you live there in the neighborhood?" He repeated the address for my witness, not once, but twice. "Now Willie Farr's lawyer there, he asked you about that address, but he didn't ask you what you did. Do you work for Mr. Farr or one of his friends or associates?"

"No sir."

"But you claim to live in a part of this city that we've already shown, in the prosecution's case, is almost all black?"

"Yes."

"And I suppose then that you work in that neighborhood," the deputy said, knowing that most of the labor in the area was either in a bar or in drugs sold on the street.

"Yes. I work there."

"What exactly is it you do, Mr. Smith?"

"I'm a priest, sir. I'm a Catholic priest. I was ordained two years ago after graduating from a seminary in southern Indiana. I'm now, and have been for almost a year, the parish priest for the neighborhood where I said I lived."

Willie had lightly kicked me under the table and I'd hid my smile behind a cough. Sometimes there were days the law could be fun.

I'd purposely picked a lot of Catholics for the jury. They weren't out very long before bringing back their "not guilty" verdict.

I smiled at the memory. Willie smiled also.

I said, "Tell me what you've heard and can tell."

"There's not that much, but the word is that you were the contract. It may just be smart talk, because the guy who was supposed to do you is dead. When you laid into that guy and Harlan Roberts blew him away then my part of town, where you and Harlan are folk heroes, thought it was okay. All I heard bad was that some said your assassin or Harlan should have knocked off Duke Theotokopolis, Ace Wing and Deuce Taylor for it to have been a good, useful party."

"Why would people feel that way?"

"Duke's had interests down in black town for years. He sells hot stuff and he don't tell people it's hot. That causes friction. Ace and Deuce used to solicit for silver when the price was high. They passed out some bad checks and then took their time in straightening things out. In other words they used the money from the silver to pay off their cold checks." He shook his head. "People who ought to know think you're still hot, Al."

83

"There's someone else out there looking?"

"They say there is."

"Why me? And do you have any idea who would be looking for me?"

"I don't know any more than what I've said. No one knows. But there have been phone calls about you to people who talk for a living, calls wanting to know where you go, promising anonymous dollars to people for information furnished. It's the way things happen when there's a contract still out."

"I keep looking. There's never anyone behind."

"Then they already know your routine."

I thought hard for a moment, feeling persons unknown walking on my grave, making me quiver inside.

"What else is going on?"

"A lot of usual things. Drug shipments loading and offloading on the river. A couple of boiler room operations selling hot cars. I hear about someone trying to fix a state lottery upriver in Illinois. And I sold a bunch of guns recent like."

Guns fit with death. "How did that happen?"

"Usual thing. I got a call from a man. He gave me a number to call back. I went to a pay phone and called him. My bet is he answered at another pay phone. He wanted six Uzis. Lots of firepower. I laid three thousand each on him and he didn't even hesitate. The next morning, by messenger, I got $18,000 cash in old-hundred-dollar bills. I delivered that night. A car came past and picked me up. I went to a place I'd stored the guns and picked them up. I put the guns in the backseat of the car I was in and another car brought me back here."

"Uzis?"

"Yeah. Small, machine pistols. Israeli issue. Very simple to use and very mean. Lots of fire power."

"You don't know who your buyer was?"

He shook his head. "I got no idea. All I heard was a voice on the phone. All I saw was a white dude driving a car. I think he had on a wig and fake glasses. I didn't make him. Probably hired for just what he did that night. Out of town and long gone by now. The price was for the guns and five clips each. Good business for me. I made some dollars. The Uzis were stolen and came to me at five hundred a crack, but I've had the storage of them for a while and that can be a chore."

"Revolutionaries? Terrorists?"

He shrugged. *Unknown.*

"What else?"

"The guy who bought the guns also wanted dynamite, but I don't deal in explosives these days. Others do, but I don't sell them anymore. My guess is the buyer would buy that the same way he bought my guns. Quiet and quick, cash up front."

"Guess on it for me, Willie."

He sat back in his chair, thinking. He used his strong right hand and caressed the trunk of a small tree that grew out of a pot beside him.

I was now sweating profusely, the back of my shirt wet through and sticking to the chair.

"Something going down. I thought maybe a bank, but who'd need dynamite for a bank?" He shook his head. "About the only guys interested in explosives these days are terrorists. They wire it to a starter or put a lot of it where it can kill a load of people. It didn't feel like that to me, but maybe it is that."

"No ideas?"

"No. Usually I let things stay like they are, but I asked for you and for me. I thought maybe it might mean something to you what with this buy coming around the same time a contract killer showed up for you. I figure you got to know something they don't want you to know, Al. Maybe from when you were lawyering." He watched me and waited.

I shook my head. I could think of nothing.

"Maybe something will come to you," Willie said. "Just remember that I never said a word to you. Zero. Nil."

"For sure," I said.

Red picked that moment to return with drinks. I sipped at cola while Red and Willie drank hot, steaming coffee. Red watched the two of us curiously.

"If you hear anything else," I began.

Willie waved a negligent hand. "Sure. But why not get Ralph and just move in here for a few weeks. I own another condo apartment in the building behind this one. It's secure. I've used it when I had problems. It's hard to get to, the windows on the alley are too small for anyone but a dwarf to climb through, and I'd be here to guard the front. Live it out. Something will happen and you'll be alive to figure it out."

"Maybe," I said. "I'll consider it." I thought some more. "Can I ask you about some people?"

He nodded.

"Clement Johnson. He called looking for me at my old office. I defended him a couple of years back on burglary. Black kid, first adult offense, but a long juvenile record."

"I know vaguely who he is," Willie said. "I know where he hangs out. A stupid kid. Runs with others of likewise intelligence. He's been out and back in since you were his lawyer. I don't know where he is now. My bet is he'd want you for business in court, not having heard you're suspended. But I'll check him out. He ain't no contract killer, that's sure."

"Abraham and Millie Burks?"

"Abe is big time. The word around is that Millie ain't with us anymore." He sat his coffee cup on the floor and waved Red away from tidying up. "I'm a street guy. Abe is a corporation guy. I live good, he lives a better. I worry about Memphis cops. Abe would worry, if he ever does, about the IRS and maybe the DEA and FBI."

"He said he was looking for me because Millie had vanished."

"Accept it was okay. Abe has a decent reputation. But be careful. He could buy you dead easy. Maybe he's your man."

"And Ace and Deuce? Could they have hired someone to come to the poker game, kill Ralph and me, and then let them handle the stuff stolen from inside the shop?"

"Maybe, but it sounds like it's beyond them. But guys constantly try to grow bigger. It's life."

"Harlan Roberts?"

"Harlan was a cop. Somehow he's now got big money and big friends. I guess he got it okay. I don't hear nothing about it being the other way. He was reasonably straight when he was a cop. People, lots of them, like him. He bleeds the same sources I bleed."

"How's that?"

"People who talk to me talk to him. They don't tell me what Harlan's asking and they don't tell him what I'm asking."

I got up. "Thanks, Willie."

"For what? I still owe you. Tell me the priest story one more time and give me my laugh for today. How was it you found him?"

I'd told him before, but he'd obliged me on this day and so I patiently obliged him. "I hung posters all around your neighborhood. He called me because he saw one on a telephone pole."

"And you told him to wear street clothes?"

"I told him only that it could be a help. I told him the prosecutor's deputy might not believe him when he testified and might jump on him. He was, and I guess is, a bright, sharp man. I think it amused him a little to do it for you, but he could also see value in it for him and his church. He wanted you to win, mostly for you, but also for him."

"He's still down there," Willie said. "Now and then I make a small donation to his church. And we grin at each other when I pass him on the street. He's good with kids."

I nodded.

"You ever going back into the law business, Al?"

"I doubt it." I looked at my watch. Time to move on. "Who knows? I like it the way it is now. And I don't drink. I've got a date with a pretty girl in an hour or two. And I need to get out of this perspiration pit of yours and take a long, cold shower before I see her."

"Hot's good for you. Sweating will keep you healthy."

"Not me," I said. I shook his hand. Mine, despite the fact I was in shape, was sweaty, but his was warm and dry and very strong. I remembered looking over the prosecution's pictures of what he'd done to the two brawny lads who'd tried to kill him. He'd carved them like a double Thanksgiving roast. Yet in all my dealings with him he'd been as fine and cooperative a client as I'd ever had. He'd viewed the murder indictment with an amused eye, perhaps figuring that he'd gotten away with enough stuff so that being wrongly convicted still wouldn't pay the due bill.

And then he'd gotten off.

"You come back soon," he said affably. "I'll ask some more and I'll call if I hear anything." He nodded. "Red?"

Red took me back to the outside door. He took hold of my arm when we were there. "Willie has got himself into state tax troubles. I told him to tell you, but of course he wouldn't. Who should we call?"

"State tax troubles can mean IRS troubles. They cooperate," I warned. I gave him the name of the best tax man I knew. He wrote it down.

I stepped out into cool wind. Red stood inside and fanned himself.

"You guys like each other, don't you?" he asked, not certain about how to take it, whether to be jealous or amused.

"Willie's a friend."

He considered it for a moment and then, I thought, decided it was all right.

"I'll make sure he keeps checking for you, Al."

"Thank you, Red," I said gravely.

I got into the VW and drove away. Behind me Red still watched, not sure of his world or mine, maybe wondering if either worked right.

Once he'd told me, not in jest, that "AIDS killed and herpes, like love, was forever."

9

Tuesday, July 23, 6:15 P.M.

SUE HAD SAID I could come past at six. I was almost on time after taking a cooling shower.

Her television was blaring the news of the day when I pushed her doorbell.

She opened the door. She was dressed in blue. I saw again that she wasn't as tall as Judy or as striking, but she had a kind of beauty that grew on the beholder. She looked very alive and vivid and she had those extra-small curves that, I knew, would eventually drive me up a tree. Maybe this time I'd like staying in that tree and it would be my tree rather than one shared with the entertainment world.

I reflected that one of my problems with Judy was that I'd been too smart to ever fall completely in love with her because I'd known, very soon, that she didn't love me. She'd wanted me for the symbol I'd been. Big lawyer, big money rolling in. *Success.*

Sue smiled at me and I was enchanted.

"Come inside. I thought I'd cook for you, unless there was something else you wanted to do."

I'd planned on taking her to the Rendezvous, a small place off a downtown alley that serves the best ribs in Memphis, but the ribs could keep. I found I was in the mood to be domesticated.

I followed her inside. I sat on the couch while she worked in the kitchen, refusing my proffered help.

"Tell me what you've found out."

I told her some of what had happening, cautioning her that it must go no further.

"No new problems?"

"I'm not sure. Sometimes I feel like someone sly is watching me from far away. I went around a lot of corners tonight before I drove here. If there was a someone tailing me he's smarter and better than I am because there just wasn't anyone back there I could see. Maybe they know enough about my routine so as not to have to tail me. That's what Willie thought."

"You mean if there's a watcher he already knows where you're going and when?"

"It's a possibility."

She brought out her own drink and sat down at the other end of the couch, far away for now. "The solution will come to you, Al. I know that, but, like you said, why would someone buying guns also want dynamite? That's an unusual combination."

"I'm not sure. It could be to blow up a car, maybe tie six sticks onto a starter, or put lots more of it in a trunk and set it off to terrorize old Memphis. Mostly, these days, it gets used in quarries, on farms to clear land, blow out stumps of trees. Or in coal mines." I thought some more. "Uzis and dynamite. It is, as you said, an unusual combination."

"Tell me exactly what Uzis are."

"Willie Farr described them as machine pistols. I've heard of them before. They shoot a whole clip of bullets in a couple of seconds. Or you can set them to fire a single shot at a time. I don't know lots about them. I never saw one, but I recognized the name when Willie mentioned it. I guess maybe I've run across the name in the newspapers. It's an Israeli gun."

"But you never had one show up in a case you tried?"

"Not when I was sober. In other words, not that I remember."

"Did you ever defend anyone who was into guns?"

"Willie, of course. And a lot of other people I defended were people who'd know guns, use guns, and own guns."

"How about the people who are in this present affair? People you think might have something to do with what's happening?"

I shook my head. "My problem is it could be someone I've not thought of yet. Of those I do know, it could be any or all of them."

"Did you call that lawyer who held your disciplinary hearing?"

"I haven't reached him yet, but I've called. I'll try him at his home and his office tomorrow."

She was drinking something tall and reddish in color. My nose, which could smell almost all in these new, sober times, told me it was nonalcoholic.

"What is that?" I asked.

"Cream soda," she said. "I don't like alcoholic drinks that much, Al. And I got to thinking you'd taste them when you kissed me and that it might bother you."

"No. When I kissed you the other night it didn't bother me. I swear I liked it a whole bunch." I didn't tell her I'd been afraid the first time I'd kissed a girl who'd been drinking. That had been pre-Sue, post-Judy.

"Let's still see if this way works even better," she said.

"I hope that's an invitation?"

She nodded shyly. "It's an hour to dinner. And we've nothing to do but wait for things to finish in the oven."

"Come with me," I said.

More enthusiasm on her part led to gentle experimentation on mine. *Better.*

The food was first class when we got to it later. Swiss steak, tender carrots, and small, new potatoes cooked under a tomato and onion cover. Good.

I went home and slept soundly after Sue shooed me out before midnight.

• • •

IN THE WARM morning I was going through the shop mail when Ralph came downstairs with a handsome, hand-tooled box under his arm.

"What's that?"

"Walter Blankenship," he answered as if that was an entire explanation. He placed the lovely box on the counter and regarded it. "He called last night late and said he wanted to sell his collection. I knew what he'd paid for it and so I made him a pass and he took me up on it. He dropped this by early this morning and I gave him a check. Since then I've been on the phone to New York City and I think I've sold it for a decent profit."

"And Walter Blankenship sold it to you just like that? No other bids, no dickering?" I knew that Ralph had spent years helping the eccentric Blankenship acquire an almost unparalleled collection of gold ancients, and it was incredible to me that he'd ever part with it, much less on the spur of the moment. Now and then Blankenship would enter the shop, talk animatedly to whoever was there of the collection, look over a few things with hauteur, and then depart.

An odd duck pain-in-the-butt.

"Just like that," Ralph answered in high good humor. "I warned him I'd sell his collection before noon today and he said he didn't care one whit. "Coins," he continued, raising his voice a full octave and speaking in a recognizable imitation of Blankenship's languid drawl, "are cold and lifeless and colorless and dull." He raised the tooled-leather lid. "My, my. These sure are pretties to be cold and dull."

"Yeah, sure," I said, gazing with wonder at the lovely array of ancient gold rarities, enough to buy a small kingdom or a four-bath Germantown house. The coins were nestled securely in rows inside their custom plastic holder. I'd seen some of the more recent pieces as they'd come through the shop individually, but I'd never seen the entire collection together and the effect was stunning. The total value had to be astronomical. Hell, the box alone was probably worth more than my Dasher.

"There has to be more to it than that." I raised my eyes from Blankenship's lovelies. "What's he into now. Stamps? Gems?"

"Butterflies," Ralph said. He laughed a small, hurt laugh.

"You're kidding me."

"Nope. That's what he told me." Ralph cleared his throat for the effort and then continued in Blankenship's voice. "Butterflies are the handiwork of God with Nature, unsullied by degrading human artifice. The rest of the world, these coins included, is feces."

"Christ," I said, unbelievingly.

"Him, too, apparently," Ralph said, with a shake of his head. "Walter reminds me of a character in a book I read as a child. I can't remember the title, but the book was about a bunch of animals. They dressed and talked like human beings. One of them was a wealthy toad who rushed from one hobby to another, abandoning each as something different caught his attention."

The Wind in the Willows," I said, laughing at the aptness of Ralph's parallel. "You're right. Walter's a perfect toad."

I opened the last few pieces of mail while Ralph took one more look and then put the tooled box in the safe. When he was done doing that I said, "That note I guess you bought for Harlan did come in the mail." I looked it over quickly. It was a 1902 Holbrook Arizona blue seal.

Ralph took it from me. He held the clear plastic bill holder, note inside, to the light, examining it, checking corners, folds, and signatures. After a few moments, punctuated by approving grunts, he looked up at me and smiled. "I'd call it extra fine, probably pressed at one time or another, but essentially unscathed and unmolested. A very nice piece."

"You want me to call Harlan?"

"Yes. You do it."

I telephoned Roberts Security Service. I gave my name and business to a switchboard operator and got through to Harlan right away.

"Al Sears, Harlan."

He sounded cautious when he answered. "Hello, Al. What can I do for you?"

"Well, I don't have anyone I need you to shoot off my back today."

He laughed tentatively. "Call me when you do. I lose little sleep over dead scumbags."

"Agreed," I said. "Coin shop business today, Harlan. I've got something for you to see."

"Ralph has been promising me something new. A Nevada or an Arizona? From a small town?"

"How about a 1902 Holbrook Arizona in extra-fine?"

"Great!" Harlan's voice had changed. "I want to see it soonest."

"I'll deliver it."

"I have to go back to the house for papers I forgot. I'm leaving here in a little bit. Could you meet me at the house, bringing the note?"

"Sure. Let me make sure by asking Ralph."

Ralph nodded agreeably.

"What time?"

"Someone's with me now on business. How about, say ten-thirty? You know my address?"

"I think I know where you live. If not, Ralph will know."

I hung up.

Ralph smiled, having heard my side of the conversation. "Sounds eager. That's how I like my customers." He lifted the bill and inspected it once more. "My bet is you have a new home." He looked up at the wall clock. "I ought to wrap Walter Blankenship's coins and have you drop them off at the airport freight terminal. I promised the man I called in New York City that I'd ship today. Pickup service might make it, but if you could find the time?"

I nodded. "I can find it. I'll deliver the note to Harlan and then go on to the airport. I want to spend a little time with Harlan and ask him some questions."

"Okay with me. I called him the other day when I got the note sent on approval and he said some things about Benny. You might ask him about that. He never liked Benny, a feeling shared by many."

"What exactly did he say?"

"He said Benny had cheated and stolen from enough bad people he was surprised he'd lived as long as he had." Ralph grinned. "He kept referring to Benny as 'that flatheaded thief.' "

"Maybe Harlan will have something new."

Ralph nodded carefully and went to the safe.

When I left the shop some twenty minutes later I took with me the Arizona note in my inner coat pocket and the tooled box, now securely wrapped. I placed the box in the trunk of the Dasher.

Outside it was that time of day when the city's traffic was light. Even the highest-paid executives in Memphis have arrived at work by midmorning, and it was still too early for the midday lunch scramble. I made good time on Poplar, so I slowed and killed a few moments driving through the shady lanes of Overton Park.

The park is one of the gems of Memphis, acre upon acre of well-kept woods and lawns, with enough room left over to accommodate a golf course, several playgrounds and swimming pools, dozens of picnic areas, an Academy of Arts, and the best zoo south of St. Louis. A few years back the forces of what's laughingly called progress tried to run an expressway through the center of the park. A bunch of diehards fought them in zoning meetings and in the courts to preserve the park. To the surprise of the city, the diehards had so far been successful, and the park remained undivided by concrete. Of course our Memphis traffic problems had continued to worsen . . .

Harlan inhabited a stately old mansion on a short street that dead-ended into the side of Overton Park, not a hundred yards from the zoo. Though there was no shortage of trees near that cul-de-sac, they were all doing their stately guard duty close to the houses, and there was no shade to be had along the street. I was still five minutes early, so I turned the Dasher around and drove back around the corner and found shade there. Although it was midmorning, it was already hot outside. A bright gold-piece sun shone in a cloudless sky.

I figured it would get hotter.

I had no intention of leaving the car with the package of coins in the trunk. It's something done only by crazies and damned fools. One never knows who has followed and is watching and waiting. Coins are valuable and very portable. Thieves and robbers abound.

I opened the trunk and took the small, heavy package with me. It was probably as safe in the trunk as it would be with me in Harlan's house, but if I'd had the car under guard I'd still not have left six figures in coins in a car trunk.

Harlan must have been watching for me, because he opened the door himself as I came up the broad, marble steps.

"Come inside, Al," he said. He held wide the huge front door and let out enough air-conditioning to cool my apartment for a week. "What else is that you're carrying?"

"Just coins to drop at the airport. No paper."

He nodded and lost interest. Coins didn't affect him. I followed him down a long hall and into a large room that was obviously his office/study.

"Your air-conditioning is very efficient."

"Yeah," he said, smiling. He waved me to a chair. "From the size of the utility bills I can't shut the house down for summer vacation for fear of causing layoffs at Memphis Light, Gas and Water."

He sat down himself, sitting forward in the chair with his elbows on his knees and rubbing his hands briskly together. "Let me see it."

I put my heavy package down beside my chair and took the clear plastic holder from my shirt pocket and handed it across to him.

He examined the note as closely as Ralph had. He lifted it out of the plastic billholder and turned it this way and that. Then he looked up at me with a smile. "Ralph was right, Al. Let me get you a check."

He got up and went to his desk. He put the old bill in its holder down carefully on the blotter while he rummaged through the flat center drawer.

"Damn, damn," he said softly. "I must have left my personal checkbook in my carry bag when I got back from Atlanta. Wait and I'll go find it."

"No huge rush, Harlan," I said. "You can drop us a check in the mail."

"You'll never make a good coin dealer if you encourage customers not to pay their bills on delivery," he said with a smile. "Hasn't Ralph taught you the fundamentals of dealing? Get the money up front. You wait. I'll be right back." He left the room.

He'd been gone only moments when the phone on his desk rang. It rang only once more before falling silent, so I assumed Harlan or another member of his family or staff had answered on an extension.

I had a notion to listen in, but I controlled myself. It wasn't that I had no curiosity, but I didn't want to get caught.

I WAITED. HARLAN was gone for ten or fifteen minutes more. I spent the time admiring his office and its accouterments, especially a framed denomination set of six crisp 1896 Educational notes, three obverses, three reverses, one, two, and five dollars, all crisp unc. They were encased in glass under pressure on the wall behind his desk. I also looked over a very fine Tennessee First Charter National ten-dollar note, Series 1875, Memphis. I was nose to glass with it, absorbed in thinking on its possible history, when Harlan returned.

"Sorry to take so long," he said, handing me the check. "The call was from my office, a minor crisis there no one would take the initiative on. Help's tough to find these days." He looked me over as he spoke. "You can get lots of semiskilled trench soldiers who want to know what the benefits are and how long is vacation. You can find no command help."

I waited and listened.

"All I have to do is work seventy hours a week and hope things don't screw up too badly in the hours when I'm not working."

"Sounds like a bad problem."

"It is." He looked me over some more. "I called a lawyer I know and can tolerate to get a second opinion on you. He says you're medium smart if your brain ain't all the way pickled in alcohol. Is it, Al?"

"I hope not. I drank for a while and I drank a lot. Physically I feel good and I can't sense any problems. Mentally I don't have anything to compare with because I'm not doing the kind of work I once did. I can't say for sure that alcohol didn't do me some damage. Now and then I seem not to remember things I ought to remember."

"Would you ever consider a job working for someone else? Someone like me?"

"I don't know. I'd talk," I said, flattered.

"Would it bother you to work under someone who grew up in the dirty, black streets and whose great-grandfather was a field slave?"

"No."

"Maybe you could do the job for me." He smiled, almost to himself, a fleeting thing. "I both disliked and admired you when you were a lawyer. Ralph likes you. I trust Ralph. He says you're all the way off the booze and he also said he's paying you half a fee on that guy we partnered to kill."

"I still get the urge to drop away from coins and go back to the bars," I said.

"Well, dry I could maybe use you. Wet, you were never much. Think on working for me. Will you do that?"

"I sure will and I'm flattered you thought of me. Now can I pick your brain a bit on that guy who died at the card game?"

He nodded.

"Do you know Abe Burks?"

"Sure. He's a true big operator. He's into high things and, at his level, they're only slightly illegal. There was a rumble on him not too long ago downtown. His wife disappeared and the state and sheriff thought he did it. Abe picked her out of a Vegas chorus line ten years or so back." He shook his head. "I guess maybe he could have killed her in a rage or something. But he wouldn't have had to. If he was *really* mad at her he'd have made a little night call and someone would have come and driven her south of the border down Mexico way. She'd be diddling herself to death now in one of a hundred places where Abe and friends have a minority interest. Or he'd have put her on a boat to Hong Kong or someplace. He's the kind of bastard who'd surely have done that rather than just let her off the hook by killing her. That's unless he was in a rage. Abe hates good." He shrugged. "Other than that Abe ain't a bad guy."

"She was buying gold coins," I said. "Ace and Deuce were involved some way."

He nodded. "I saw her around a few area coin shows, gold shopping, maybe man shopping. She was more woman that Abe needed, one hot lady and thirty years younger than him."

"It's told when she left she took the gold coins with her. I've got a list of the pieces. It's a collection of one major gold coin from each country, past or present. Some very good stuff. Would seeing the list mean anything to you?"

"No. I was never into gold."

"Could Ace or Deuce be more than I think they are?"

"I don't know. They live poor, but I've known people who did that who could buy hotel chains. If a man will steal nickels he might also plan on breaking into Fort Knox."

"How about Duke?"

"He's your buddy, not mine. A clever man and very arrogant and snobbish one for what he actually is—and that's a con man. He's an opportunist with a big ego."

"You don't like him?"

"Let's say I know him. Knowing him makes him difficult to love. He's a man who thinks he can talk anyone into anything at any time."

I smiled. The description was apt.

"What do you hear about Benny?"

"Nothing. It went down strictly as a mugging. It probably was, but then it happened about the same time you tackled a shooting target for me. That makes it peculiar. Call Smitty. You know him. I'll call him also and tell him to be open with you. He may and then, again, he may not."

"Thank you."

"That's enough for now." He got up from the chair, seemingly tired of the conversation. "I won't offer you a real drink," he said, watching me closely. "It's still too early in the day to drink anyway, and I don't want to be the one who starts you up again."

"I hope no one ever starts me again."

"Hoorah for you. It's too hot for coffee outside and I've got to go back into the heat and so do you. But maybe something else. How about a bottle of pop?"

I declined politely, but he insisted, so I said, "All right. A diet cola if you've got it."

He went around to the other side of his desk, depressed a switch, and gave the order into a sophisticated instrument that would not have looked out of place on the bridge of the starship *Enterprise*. "Yes," he repeated into the phone. "Bring the drinks to us in the basement shooting gallery."

"Follow me," he ordered, enjoying himself being lord of the manor.

He led me out and through the huge hall of the house. In an alcove, behind thick curtains, there were double doors. He opened them and turned on lights. Marble steps led down to a lower floor. The smell of the place, once we were down, was slightly musty. There was a massive old-fashioned billiard table in a room we passed. In another, though an ajar door, I could see expensive exercise equipment.

A final door opened to a shooting gallery. Harlan pushed on lights and there were targets about forty feet away. They seemed fastened to a solid wall.

"Sand bags behind the targets," he said laconically. He used a key and opened a heavy wood cabiniet. "You want to take a try at a target with this revolver?"

"I told you earlier I'm not much for guns. Just never could use them. About the best I've done with weapons was when I was younger. I bow hunted a little then."

An elegant looking, middle-aged light black woman appeared at the door. She set frosty bottles, a bucket of ice, and glasses, all on a silver tray, on the shooting counter. She gave us a look of disapproval and wasted no time starting her return trip.

"Thank you, Wilma," Harlan said to her retreating back. She gave no indication of having heard.

I raised an inquiring eyebrow.

Harlan smiled. "Wilma worked for the Rasmussens for twenty years before they sold this house and moved on to Switzerland. They tried everything to get her to go with them. She has family here in Memphis and so she stayed. I then offered to keep her on as housekeeper at the same salary she was paid by the Rasmussens and since then we've been in close combat." He shook his head. "You see she knows I'm basically a field hand. But my wife lives in fear she'll leave us for someone else. She's always after me to increase Wilma's salary or give her some added perks." He lifted a bottle from the tray and, disdaining ice or glass, he drank from it. I followed suit from a diet cola bottle. "I told her to bring bottles only. The ice and glasses and tray were her additions." He shook his head. "In a way I love her and she knows it."

He sat his bottle down on the tray and waited until I'd done the same.

"Ralph says and I remember you used to be in gymnastics. How come you have trouble with guns?"

"I'm not sure. A cop tried to teach me, once. He said I couldn't make it work because I couldn't figure out the relationship between my hands, the gun, and a target. Anyway, I was a true dud at it." I smiled. "He told me to throw big rocks instead of carrying a gun."

He handed me a revolver. It was large, but seemed light weight.

"Twenty-two on a .45 frame. Show me how you'd try to aim it?"

I pointed it down toward the targets, trying to eye line one of them up. The gun felt awkward in my hand.

"Do you see all right?"

"I guess. I'm slightly astigmatic and glasses seem to compound it. I don't have any trouble with normal things and I can read any chart known. Things that are close are easier for me."

Harlan took the gun back. "Let's try something based on the fact that your hand would be nearer to you than that target down there. I'm going to load some .22 shorts in this pistol and then show you how to fire it. It isn't the way you were taught to do it before. Want to give it a try?"

"Sure," I said, humoring him.

He put small cartridges in the gun and handed it to me. "Take your index finger off the trigger and use your second finger on that trigger. Lay your index finger below the cylinder as if it was what you were aiming. Then point your finger at a target on the wall and fire.

I did. The revolver made a little pop. I was pointing my finger at the center target on the wall.

"Do it again. Then once more," Harlan ordered.

I fired until the shells were gone.

Harlan whistled a tuneless melody to himself and went up for the target. He returned it and handed it to me.

There were seven holes in it, most of them very near the black bull's-eye.

"Works for some people," Harlan said.

"Lord, lord. I never could do much good with any kind of target before."

Harlan seemed pleased that I was pleased.

"Try it again," he said, reloading.

I did, with similar results.

Harlan took the gun and popped the spent cartridges. "There's a legend that this is how Billy the Kid shot. I don't know whether it's true or not, but that's the story." He gave me a long look. "You should carry a gun what with the pickle you're in."

"If anything else happens then I might," I said.

"If anything else happens," he said softly. "It could be way too late. You want to borrow this gun?"

"That would be very good of you."

He reloaded it once more, this time with longer cartridges. He found a cardboard box to fit it and put it inside the box after wrapping the gun in oiled paper.

"Carry it," he ordered.

I hefted the package off the floor. "Could we go upstairs now? I should head for the airport. Time flies and this keeps getting heavier. But I thank you for the lesson and the loan of the gun." I nodded. "Billy the Kid, huh?"

"Yep."

"Me and Billy."

"Think more on working for me. No booze."

"Positively."

We went upstairs. He saw me to the door and I made my way down his walk. The flower beds were carefully tended and the bushes were trimmed. I looked back at the door of the huge million-dollar house, but Harlan had already vanished back inside.

IO

BY THE GENEVE wristwatch I wore I noticed it was 11:30. I opened the VW trunk again and placed the coin package back inside, snugged it against the spare tire, ready for airport delivery. I then closed the trunk.

The trees overhead had provided decent shade and I'd left the driver's side window down, but it was now uncomfortably hot outside. I started the engine and turned the air-conditioning up from low to max-fan-cool and rolled up the window.

The air conditioner on the Dasher was one of the few things that still worked well. I now had the money to get the car worked over, but had not yet gotten around to it. Maybe I was still punishing myself for the lost Mercedes that Judy had taken. That thought made me smile. It had never been my car.

Whatever their faults, the Memphis expressways are better than no expressways at all. A trip from midtown to the airport can take half an hour longer using city streets (with no telling *how* long it would take if the bulk of the traffic wasn't being carried on the expressways), but you can get on the expressway at Union and get off at the airport ten minutes later, except during peak rush hours.

I pulled into the fast lane after completing the 270-degree

turn to the right, which put me on I-240 heading south. Traffic was prenoon light. The car had cooled some and I started my left hand in a motion to turn the air conditioner down a notch when a movement on the floor on the passenger's side caught my eye. I glanced downward and caught a glimpse of something dark pulling back beneath the seat. I stopped moving and waited and watched. In a moment my curiosity was answered when a dark brown head and bright, glassy eyes darted out again, followed by several feet of slowly twisting snake.

After an indecisive moment, my heart decided it wouldn't quit on me, and then kept pumping at about twice its normal rate. That made my every move jerky. I tried to calm myself as I concentrated on maintaining control of the car with minimum movement.

Things slowed within me. I'd read somewhere that mankind's fear of snakes is a learned response rather than an instinct, and maybe that's right. During one summer of my youth I'd assembled a large, live collection of most of the nonpoisonous snakes found in the area of Tennessee hill county I'd grown up in. I'd kept them until one afternoon when my unsuspecting mother came across the cases where I'd hidden them in a seldom-used shed. After that I operated under strict orders to confine my reptile studies to the field. That had been long ago, but I remembered some things from handling those snakes and from hours spent in thumbing through the high school library's copy of Ditmar's *Reptiles of the World*. I knew that my passenger wasn't, like me, a native midsoutherner. I also realized that, learned response or not, I was afraid.

My position was precarious. Being in a car with a snake of unknown but possibly venomous ancestry isn't high on any list of ways to spend a day—and traveling down an expressway about seventy miles an hour wasn't any help. What I wanted to do was leap out of the car. If I did that common sense told me I'd probably be killed when I smacked the roadway or a following car at a lot of feet per second. It also seemed unlikely that the snake, which appeared now to be keeping curious eyes on me from its position on the carpeted floor, would sit by and watch me go through all the motions needed to exit the car. I thought it was certain it would respond to my actions in the only instinctive way it knew to handle such things—by biting me.

And yet I couldn't drive around indefinitely. The snake would likely, sooner or later, interpret one of my driving motions as hostile.

A drop of sweat fell from my nose tip downward even though the car was now cool inside.

I tried to keep my brain working. I knew that just getting the car safely stopped wouldn't solve my problem. After that I must escape the car without being bitten.

It takes a lot of seconds to slow down in the fast, left lane at a steady, unjerky pace. I concentrated on that task. I kept working on a solution. I kept wondering why the snake had taken so long to come out from under the seat. If he'd not come out when I opened the door and entered, why had he come out minutes later when I was making only the slight movements required to operate a car with automatic transmission. I shivered as I thought about it, then realized the shiver was brought on by something other than fear. I'd sweated when I first saw the snake, but now the overefficient air conditioner was turning the sweat into ice water.

An idea came. A chance. Maybe I could get out of the car and away. And when I did then I could try to find out who'd dropped my passenger into the car.

I remembered that snakes are cold-blooded animals whose body temperature is determined by the temperature of their environment. They avoid extreme temperatures, sunning themselves on cool days and seeking the shade when it's hot. The temperature in the car had been oppressive when I got in it, and the snake had sought the coolest spot it could find—beneath the seat. When I turned the air conditioner on high the temperature in the car plummeted, and the snake had come out from under the seat to find a warmer spot. It had settled on the dark carpet in front of the passenger's seat, which now was bathed in intermittent sunshine. If I could somehow manage to make it appreciably warmer in the backseat than in front, the snake might slither back, and with the seat between us I figured I had a decent chance of opening the door and exiting the car before it could get to me. It seemed worth a try, but the problem was that the snake might now be contemplating getting up on the sunbathed seat beside me. Once it was there, it was unlikely anything would make it move, and I'd not have any chance of getting out with it nestled right beside me.

The air conditioner was doing its job, and I knew that if I left it at its present setting—and I wasn't going to attract the snake's unwanted attention by reaching out and changing it—it would soon be like a frozen-food locker inside the car.

By now the car's speed had diminished by half and I was getting close to a street overpass. Cars blared their horns at slowpoke me in the left fast lane, but managed to get around. If I could manage to stop the car in the median so that the front seat was in shade and the back in sunlight that might do the job. However, that would require me to shift my right foot from the accelerator to the brake pedal quickly, and there was a good chance the snake would quickly react to that movement. I decided to try using my left foot on the brake pedal, hoping that most of its movements would be hidden from the snake by my right leg.

It worked; at least the snake didn't strike as I got my foot on the pedal and began to apply pressure. Slowly the car approached the overhead bridge and its shadow and I pulled off the left lane and onto the grassy median. The car was nearly stopped when the shadow crept up the hood and slid slowly toward me. Out of the right corner of my eye I watched until shade covered the passenger seat and climbed up to the top of the seat back. Then, with heavier pressure, I stopped the car altogether. Cars and trucks passing by continued to honk their horns in derision, but with me off the road traffic was getting back up to normal speed again.

I kept my left foot on the brake pedal so the automatic transmission couldn't start the car moving. Now it was a matter of waiting and hoping that the now-shaded snake cooled enough to seek warmth. For a long moment, in the thinking and hoping, I wondered if my own body would now be the warmest thing in the snake's vicinity.

The snake seemed content to lie on the dark carpet beside me. It appeared indifferent to the random swooshing sounds of passing cars and the light rocking motion they set up in the Dasher. I waited and hoped that the sun would soon coax my unwelcome neighbor into the back when I saw that the shadow, which I'd perched atop the back of the seat, had fallen into the back of the car and was moving steadily rearward. I'd failed to take into account that the sun would not stand still while the snake and I played out our game of fang roulette. At the rate the shadow was moving I figured I had maybe fifteen minutes more of sun and then everything in the car would cool down rapidly unless I took further action.

My body would remain an inviting 98.6 degrees . . .

I had turned my head slowly until I was looking at the snake full on. Finally, when I'd decided to take my chances and try to escape with the snake there beside me, it began to crawl under the seat, headed hopefully for the heated carpet and upholstery in the rear.

I still needed to get the car's transmission into park to keep it from maybe driving back into the left lane of the roadway and precipitating a pileup. I then must open the door and lever myself quickly out of the car. VW's have an automatic seat belt from door to center. It would open as I opened the door. I figured to give the snake a few minutes to settle into the rear before trying to accomplish all that I must do, but the snake's tail had barely disappeared when another development made my exit from the car more pressing.

A gumballed squad car, bearing two uniformed city cops, pulled in beside me. The frowning driver was writing down my license plate number. I was in the median and that was unlawful. I watched and then saw him open his door. If he got to my window I'd have a snake in the back and an officer outside.

I went for it.

I slammed the gearshift into park, hit the door with my shoulder, and pulled the door handle all at one time. The door sprang fully open. I rolled out and caught my right ankle on the door as it sprang back. There was excruciating pain, but I ignored it. I kicked at the door with both feet to get it closed before the snake could follow me onto the grassy median.

The young cop had stopped short when I burst from the car. He stood watching me. At the passenger door of the police car the other officer uncertainly drew his pistol.

With the door slammed shut I lay still, breathing hard.

The closest officer stood with his hands on hips and his feet apart.

"Not nuts, officer," I said, when my breathing slowed enough to make me able. "I swear to you there's a snake loose inside my car."

11

Wednesday, July 24, 12:14 P.M.

I-240 BECAME MESSY because of me and the police car. Memphis drivers are like all drivers. Although my car and the police car behind it were well off the roadway into the median, every driver passing slowed down to gawk. After determining there were no smashed cars or bloody bodies the interstate drivers would resume normal speed, but the effect was to jam up noontime traffic for as far back as I could see.

Eventually a pickup with OVERTON PARK ZOO stenciled on its side detached itself from the sluggish stream of traffic and pulled in behind the police car. A tall, thin black man wearing a dark green uniform got out and came to where one of the policemen and I stood near my car. The other policeman, the one who'd stayed by the car while his partner approached me, was back inside the patrol car again, speaking to someone on the radio.

"Where is it?" the black man asked. He was young, and the name Russell was stitched in red thread above his shirt pocket.

"Mr. Russell," the cop began, "we got something here I never ran into before—snake problems."

"Just Russell," the black man said. "Not Mr. Russell. The name's Russell Jones."

"I'm Officer Ted Bryant," the cop said politely. "This gentleman is Allan Sears. He's the one with the snake in his car."

"You're the zoo's herpetologist?" I asked as we shook hands.

"Sort of. I take care of the poisonous snakes. Where's the snake now?"

I took him to the driver's side of my car and pointed through the rear window. The snake nestled serenely in the still partial sunlight of the rear seat.

A smile split Jones's face and made him seem younger. "That's Wilbur all right."

The policeman and I exchanged amused glances. Officer Bryant asked, "You call the snake Wilbur?"

"That's what he's called," Russell Jones answered. "He was reported missing and we've been looking for him for about an hour." He turned to me. "How'd he get inside your car?"

"That's what I'd like to find out. I was parked for a while a block or so from the zoo. Then, when I was driving down the expressway, he poked his snout and the rest of him out from under the passenger's seat."

Russell smiled. "Must have given you a scare, but Wilbur, he's usually docile."

"You mean he's not poisonous?"

"He's poisonous. Kraits are among the most poisonous snakes. But Wilbur isn't aggressive. You might have been safe driving with him in your car, assuming you didn't step on him or make him feel threatened. Slow and easy by you would have kept him easy and slow. Now a black mamba or a taipan would be an entirely different story. Those honeys are even-tempered. By that I mean they're mad and mean all the time."

I looked at my watch. I still had questions to ask. "Listen, er—Russell. I'd like to talk more with you, but I've got a package to get to the airport. Could you take your Wilbur home to the zoo and meet me somewhere later for lunch?"

"You doing the buying?"

"Sure. I'll buy."

"Then how about Armand's? Say one-thirty? Their lunch crowd should have thinned out enough by then."

"Great. I'll be there."

"Okay," he said. He became briskly professional. "Why don't you gents clear away from the door and let me fetch Wilbur out of there." Which he proceeded to do with a minimum of fuss, skillfully using a stick with a leather loop on its end to lift Wilbur out of my car and into a heavy cloth bag.

When the snake was on its way back to the zoo, I asked Officer Bryant if I was free to go.

"I suppose," he said. "Putting a poisonous snake into someone's car could be attempted murder. I'm thinking we ought to impound the car."

"I doubt that would do any good. Someone throwing in a snake isn't likely to leave fingerprints. He'd just drop the snake through a window. They were open earlier. I'll tell you what I can do: I can come past police headquarters this afternoon and talk to your Detective Smith. He knows me. I want to find out what's going on also, but, for now, maybe it was a prank. Or maybe Wilbur crawled in by himself."

Officer Bryant wasn't convinced, but, after making me promise again to contact Detective Smith, he let me go. I drove on to the airport and got the package receipted and insured and into transit.

I watched around me. There was, as always, no one.

ARMAND'S WAS ONE of several restaurants that had opened up on Madison near Cooper in the nineteen seventies. Collectively, they were known as Overton Square. Food at Armand's, as at the other restaurants, was passable and pricey. You paid a little more for drinks so that you could say you'd lunched in Overton Square. For certain crowds, it was an "in" place to eat and drink. That was the usual reason I used for not going there. My appetite, seldom robust after too many years of alcohol, spoils completely when it has to eat in the company of people whose principal aim is not eating, but in seeing and being seen.

I arrived first. I was sipping a two-dollar glass of Pepsi when Russell Jones entered. I motioned him over. I was prepared for him to order the most expensive item on the menu, but he surprised me by ordering a large chef's salad and a light beer. I duplicated his salad order and added iced tea. We did small talk about the weather and Armand's and then got down to the business I wanted to pursue.

"Wilbur make it home okay?"

"Sure," Russell replied. "No worse for wear. Now he's installed in temporary quarters."

"How's that?"

"Well, the glass is broken out where he was."

"Back up. Someone broke the glass and that's how Wilbur made it out to freedom and my VW?"

Our pretty, light brown waitress, attired in a frilly pseudo-French-maid outfit with a dainty white apron and minuscule black dress that left only fractions and finals to the imagination, chose that moment to deliver our salads.

After we jointly gave her departing rear the attention it deserved, Russell dived into his salad and I had to repeat my question. His answer, slightly lettuce muffled, was intelligible.

"Okay. Case report. Sometime before eleven this morning, someone took a fire axe off the wall and broke out the glass in front of Wilbur's cage. After that Wilbur either escaped or was snakenapped."

"Do you know if anyone around the zoo saw anything?"

"I guess not. I'd have heard if someone had. The Reptile House is closed this week for cleaning and repairs. We're short-handed—the city is having trouble meeting the payroll for things like fire and police protection. Right now we get no sympathy at city hall. The workmen who should have been doing the cleaning and repairs were helping with the mess left from a small fire in the main concession center last night."

113

"Arson?"

"I don't know, but it's not likely. More probably someone dropped a cigarette in a refuse container near the south wall and it smouldered awhile and then caught things. The wood in some of the walls gets very dry in this weather."

"So someone maybe walked into the Reptile House and stole Wilbur without being challenged or seen?"

"I guess it happened that way. There were signs up saying the House was closed for all day, but I heard the workmen expected to get back to the snake job this afternoon."

I watched him mangle the salad for a minute while I mulled over what he'd said.

There seemed to be little doubt that putting the snake in my car had been another attempt to kill me. The question was how had it been set up. I'd not known myself that I was going to be at Harlan's, and within easy range of the Reptile House until a few minutes before I'd left the coin shop. Nobody else knew it either, except for Ralph, early, and Harlan, late.

Someone had been watching. That person or persons had then conceived the idea of dropping a poisonous snake in my car, gotten into the zoo, found Wilbur, and dropped him in my car. That had all been done in the space of the minutes I'd spent with Harlan. I doubted that the fire had been deliberately set, at least for use against me. An accidental fire.

Someone had waited and watched and was still waiting and watching. Someone who knew me and knew my ways.

I continued to pump Russell. I told him about the snake period of my childhood. I asked him about poisonous snakes and listened to him meander, hoping I'd hear something that might help.

He kept eating. Before long, however, he reached the bottom of the bowl and started looking at his watch. Preoccupied with my questioning I'd not touched my salad, so to keep him from running off I offered it to him. Armand's chef's salads are large and Russell was thin, but he accepted and fell on the second salad as though the first was only a dim memory.

I nibbled a spare cracker while I watched him. I resumed my questioning. By the time he staggered out Armand's front door he was full of lettuce and I was full of more information about the Overton Park Zoo than I had use for.

"YOU'RE KIDDING ME. This snake guy ate two of Armand's chef's salads? *Two* of them?" Ralph asked in wonder when I gave him a rundown on why I was so late getting back to the shop. The incident of the snake had upset him, of course, but it was past. It was now Russell's huge capacity for green leaves that had his attention.

I nodded. "One on you, one on me." I wasn't feeling very kindly toward the hungry herpetologist. On the way back to the shop I'd wolfed down a cardboardburger from one of the fast-food places and it and my stomach were having trouble becoming friendly. That might be partly because I kept remembering the snake.

"I'd have paid for both meals to have seen it," Ralph said, awe in his voice. Ralph loved to eat, but salads didn't agree with him, just as some fried foods don't agree with me. He derived a vicarious sort of pleasure out of seeing others do what he didn't want to do.

"I wish you could have watched instead of me. He took my salad on like a paratrooper."

Ralph grinned again, and then turned serious. "I think that settles things, then."

"What's settled?"

"Who that man who broke in my poker game upstairs was after."

"Me, you mean?"

"Sure."

"How about, for now, it could still me me *and* you. Just because someone was watching and tried for me alone today doesn't mean you ought to change your way of life for a while yet. We need more answers. Besides, I'm not costing you much.

And our upstairs assassin was going to take both of us with him."

He shook his head. "Sure, but it's you, Al. I was only an added attraction. He wanted the coins so he added me to his getaway list. I'm still in for half the cost, but it's you."

"Wait until we're positive."

"I'm getting very close to being there. This zoo and snake deal has no connection to me." He stopped for a moment and looked down at a coin he was putting in a holder. "Both of us were available to your snake-dropper all morning before you went to Harlan's house. If he wanted the both of us then he could have done something here, maybe shot at us through the window, or come inside after us. Nothing happened until you went off on your own. Then your watcher followed. Whoever did it couldn't have known Harlan's note would come in the morning mail, or that you'd then take that note to Harlan's house. Ordinarily I drop off Harlan's stuff at his office. The idea of the snake couldn't have occurred to anyone until you parked your car near Harlan's and close to the zoo. You follow me?"

"I'm trying."

"Okay. Someone wants to do you in, and he follows you. There's no way he can be sure how long you'll be away from your car. You could be gone a minute, you could be gone an hour. So do some thinking from the position of your watcher. Is there any way he would leave your car there, run the risk of losing you if you returned to it before he did, and go off into the zoo on the off chance of being able to steal a poisonous snake when nobody was looking?"

"One way," I answered. "He might have known in advance that the Reptile House was closed down for repairs, and it would be even better for him if he knew about last night's fire at the zoo."

"Exactly," Ralph continued. "And the only way he could have known those things would be for him to have a zoo connection. Or he'd have had to know enough about snakes to steal a poisonous one and get it into your car without getting bitten himself."

I thought on that for a moment. "Maybe it was on TV."

"I watch TV a lot. I don't remember seeing anything about the zoo on the local news."

"But you don't watch every channel. A fire at the zoo would have been news. There was a fire and therefore someone reported it and it was heard."

He shrugged.

"I don't think you have it straight, Ralph. You're looking at it from where you are and not factoring in other possibilities. All I can see is that someone followed, someone knew something about the zoo and something about snakes. The follower was lucky. He, she, or they didn't have to follow behind me every step. So I lost them? They could come back here and wait. Or go to my apartment. I haven't been hiding out, you know."

"Maybe you should be hiding out."

"I don't think any great knowledge of snakes was exhibited either. I quizzed Russell. He said the krait wasn't a good choice. It has a retiring nature. I got the idea from him that a person who knew snakes would have known this and would have broken out a more aggressive snake to use as a weapon. Our follower picked this particular snake because a sign on the cage front says it was extremely poisonous, according to Lettuce Russell. Let's say the sign had said the snake was also shy, which it didn't. Then maybe another snake would have been in the car and I'd not be here now."

"You're pretty cool about it," he said.

"I am now."

"No zoo connection?"

"Maybe, but probably not. Just a follower who reads the newspaper or listens to TV or visits the zoo and can put things together. Someplace there was a notice about the Reptile House closing. The follower saw it and remembered it." I looked at my watch. "I told the traffic officer I'd stop by police headquarters this afternoon. Can you spare me for what's left of the day?"

"Sure, Al." He eyed me with many misgivings. "You be damned careful, please. Watch around you. Take a gun."

"I'll watch. And Harlan loaned me a gun and taught me to shoot it."

"There," he said. "That shows you Harlan's okay. He'd not do that and be after you himself."

I nodded, not so sure. "How good a friend of yours is Harlan?"

"I've known and dealt with him a long time."

"You do business with him and you play poker with him, but does that mean he's not into something unknown to you which might benefit some way by my or your death?"

"I trust him," Ralph said. "I know his reputation. He's the smartest cop I ever knew. I got robbed here fifteen, maybe eighteen years ago. Guy come through the door with a pistol in his pocket. Harlan was a detective then. He solved it in less than twenty-four hours and got me my coins back."

"All of them?"

"Every one. I tried to give him something on the side and he got a little angry about it. Besides, he shot the guy who broke in our game upstairs."

I nodded. He was right in saying that Harlan had shot the robber, but Duke could have shot him, too. I thought that Harlan might have shot because he had to, because he saw that *this time* it wasn't going to play out right.

Today Harlan had been gone from the room, supposedly seeking a check, keeping me waiting longer than necessary for what had begun as a simple business transaction. In that time a snake had been inserted into my car, taken from a place Harlan was familiar with, or at least which he knew about, being a neighbor thereof.

Some of the time used had been spent in teaching me to shoot a gun. Was Harlan that clever?

Maybe.

Harlan had then loaned me a gun, but it was a .22. I remembered old trials. How much stopping power to a .22?

"You got a large caliber extra revolver I can borrow for a few days?" I asked Ralph.

"Sure. Take your pick. You know where they are. There's a couple more upstairs. Whichever one you take from down here I'll replace from upstairs."

I picked a long-barreled .38 without too much rust on it. I stuck it in my belt and buttoned my coat over it.

Ralph nodded approvingly. "You make sure you don't shoot yourself with it. That one there fires slightly high and a little to the right."

"Should help me straighten my shots."

THE AFTERNOON SUN beat down on me when I went out to my car. It was hot and the car was hot. I looked around me and saw traffic, people walking, people going into stores. No one seemed to be watching me.

I had the strong urge to take the new gun out of my belt, lay my index finger along the side of it as I'd been taught, and check under the seats before I got in the VW, but I resisted. Instead I sighed, opened the trunk, and let the new gun join the one Harlan had supplied. Now I was a two-gun man and I still hadn't broken myself in to carrying one of them.

I began to relax after a few blocks and concentrated on the traffic, still watching behind me, seeing nothing.

12

Wednesday, July 24, 5:30 P.M.

SMITTY WASN'T HELPFUL. He was interested, but he knew nothing new and saw little of use to him in the snake incident.

"So you dived out of the car, got away, and then later had lunch with this snake guy?" he asked, his tone neutral.

"I had some iced tea. He had his lunch and then ate mine." I waited and watched Smitty drum his pencil on the desk. I thought he was bored and it had already been a long day for both of us.

"Give us a call if anything else happens," he said politely.

"Can I ask if you ever found any connection between John Shelton and anyone in Memphis?"

"What interests you in John Shelton other than the fact you helped Harlan knock him off?"

"You said he was here in Memphis before. Who was he working for then?"

"Don't know for sure. A state senator got killed. Clean hit."

"Who locally wanted the state senator out of it?"

"Lots of people. This senator had a nasty habit of selling his vote and then finking on the sale. And every session he'd do neat little things like dropping in a bill to raise taxes on liquor, beer, and cigarettes. A couple of times he was after more taxes on motels and hotels. He wasn't serious about it, but he did get a lot of free stuff in return for letting those kinds of bills quietly drop."

"Could all these tricks have irritated the big boys? Maybe someone like Abe Burks?"

Smitty stopped doodling with his pencil and looked at me keenly. "What do you know about Abe Burks?"

"Nothing. I represented his wife once."

"I remember that." He smiled without humor. "You slicked her out of a DUI causing death charge. She's gone, vanished. We think she's dead."

"Yeah, I heard that. How about any connection between Abe and this senator?"

He shook his head, not knowing. "Possible. Abe's got some hotel ownerships and he owns a piece of some beer distributorships. But his group would have their own executioners and not use someone like The Shell, an independent contractor. Or maybe they wouldn't. Why did you think of Abe?"

"He's the only big-time name I know that I ever had anything to do with. Usually the big local crooks brought in lawyers from New York and someone local would get them admitted for the case. I represented mostly little people."

I could see Smitty was losing interest again.

"How about Benny Wilson?" I asked. "Anything new on his death?"

"I didn't have that one," Smitty said. "I heard about it is all. He got mugged in an alley."

"He was into coins," I said. "Kind of funny he'd get mugged the same night someone tried hitting Ralph and me. Whoever got him also got his coin stash, if he was packing one."

Smitty shrugged. "I like it when you explain these things to me. You're a private detective. These people you're interested in and telling me stories about, dropping names, and picking my brain, all have to do with you. *You* tell me what your ideas are."

"I haven't a single hunch. I was just wondering what yours were."

"Wonder elsewhere, please. I got a lot of reports to do."

I got up.

"Thank you for coming in," he said, overpolitely. "The officer who pulled in behind you left me a report that said you'd be in to talk to me." He shook his head, maybe relishing his thoughts. "Must have scared the hell out of you finding a snake in your car."

"I was scared," I said, remembering.

"Yeah," he said. He initialed a paper from his desk and put it into a bulky stack beside him. "I ain't Sherlock Holmes. You find out something that means something to me, something I can get my teeth in, then you come get me. I'll do my best to help. But I don't know why someone's after you or why Benny Wilson got mugged."

I left.

Outside I figured I was on my own. That didn't make me angry, but it did unsettle me a little more.

I HEARD IT ringing before I got to my apartment door. I know people who are casual about phones. They'll let theirs ring half a dozen times, staring at it angrily or apathetically, before answering. I know others who, if they're not in the mood to talk, will let the phone ring without answering it at all. I once made my living, or much of it, on the phone. Lawyers do. I'm incapable of hearing a phone ring without doing my damndest to answer it as quickly as I can.

In my haste to enter my apartment I dropped my keys and had to fumble for them on the floor before I could unlock. I slammed the door behind me and snatched up the phone at the end of my couch.

"Hello," I said, hoping my caller was still there.

"Hello, Al," was all she said, but I knew from the first syllable it was Judy. Much of the reason for her local television success was her voice. She could make it soothing or exciting or, sometimes, as cold as a tax collector. She'd used the cold voice on me exclusively during our last months together.

I hated myself for it, but the soothing, coaxing tone of today gave me a small thrill.

I didn't pretend not to know who it was.

"Hello, Judy," I said.

She waited for me to say more, but I didn't.

After a moment of silence, she said, "How've you been doing, Al. I hear you've stopped drinking."

"I'm okay," I said. "And I'm not drinking."

I thought she was surprised I wasn't fawning all over her, because she said baldly, "I didn't think you had it in you." Then the voice went soothing again. "You've shown remarkable strength in beating your drinking problem, Al."

"I can't say I've beaten it, Judy," I said. "A drunk doesn't beat alcohol. He stops drinking for a while, hopefully for all time. I'm doing the best I can." I paused. "Why did you call?"

"I need to see you, Al." There was a touch of little-girl in her voice. I got embarrassed with myself remembering that I'd once thought it was hugely cute.

"What about?"

"Maybe a part of it is just to see you, Al. To talk. We haven't seen each other for a long time. We need to talk."

"There aren't any things left for us to talk about."

"You can't mean that. We meant a lot to each other for a long time." I heard a hint of mockery in her voice now.

"Judy, we're divorced. You went to court, testified you wanted out, and got out. A judge signed the papers. I've got a copy of the decree in my top drawer. You got your maiden name back. With the exception of the VW, which I'm grateful to own, you took whatever else we didn't jointly blow or I didn't pour down me. The only thing we could talk about would be old, bad times."

"You're being cruel," she said. It was an old, used remark, one I'd heard many times before. Judy liked to think that people were being cruel to her.

"Forget about it—and about me, Judy," I said. "Nothing's left of what used to be." I waited a moment for protest and then started to hang the phone up.

I think she sensed what I was doing because she raised her voice high enough for me to hear it with the phone near the cradle.

"The chain cent!" she said.

I brought the phone back to my ear. "What did you say?"

"I said that there was the chain cent."

"What does that mean?" The 1793 chain large cent had been the best of the pieces in my almost complete type set. I'd traded a mostly uncirculated (many in high mint states) set of Morgan dollars for it and given boot. The chain cent was mint state 60 and was one of the best survivors of the series left. It could bring at least, now, a mid-five figure amount, maybe low six figures in the right auction with the right bidders. I'd always assumed it had gone the way of the rest of the collection. Judy had unloaded most of what coins were left to Ralph as soon as the ink on the decree dried. He'd dispersed it before I came to his place to work and he never, now, spoke of it to me.

"I kept it, Al. I sold the rest of the stuff, but I kept the chain. I'm not sure why. Maybe I wanted to see if it would appreciate in value like you told me it would."

"It has."

"Maybe it was more than that. Maybe it was because it once meant so much to you. Now that you're straightened out, maybe I could give it back to you?"

"No. It's yours, Judy," I said. I remembered the fever I'd been in to possess it, much like the fever I'd once been in to possess Judy. But I had only managed a leasehold without owning her, a sharing arrangement where other tenants became involved. I continued, "It was part of the settlement. It belongs to you. I promise you I drank my half."

"Please come talk to me, Al."

"There's nothing left to talk about. The coin is yours. Sell it or don't sell it. Take it to Ralph. He can tell you what it will bring and what to do with it. I just work for him."

"I want you to come talk to me about it, not Ralph," she said, her voice harder. "If you won't then I'll take it to your friend Harvey Kendall and sell it to him for whatever he offers."

That stopped me. Harvey Kendall didn't have a mask and a gun, but he was worse than many a strongarm robber I'd defended in court. Harvey operated his coin business mostly within the law, but he took every advantage he could. I knew he'd acquired coin properties by disparaging values, by thinking out loud that some of the items might be stolen (and therefore would have to be returned). I'd heard of him browbeating estate heirs into not getting a second appraisal by claiming he'd sold the items and that the deceased had promised them to him. He was shadier than an August grove of trees, and too smart to ever get himself into something where he could be found provably crooked.

Most of the bad people I'd represented as lawyer I could stomach. But I hated Harvey Kendall.

After I'd become semi-expert in coins I'd stayed away from his flashy establishment. The last time I'd heard from him was when he'd found I'd acquired the chain cent. He'd called to try to buy it from me. He'd been sweetness and light, very up front. He must have had an eager buyer waiting because he'd offered me a good profit. That had meant to me that he was going to stick it to his buyer. I didn't sell. I hadn't bought for resale. If I had I'd not have sold to good, old Harv. Most coin dealers were decent businessmen. Harv was the final exception. He was a shark and a wolf and a dragon.

I'd intimated that to him that day on the phone. Judy had heard it and asked about it. Now she remembered what I'd said about Harv.

"When do you want me to come see you?" I asked, fighting anger. I'd get in and quickly out. I'd talk her into letting Ralph either buy the coin or sell it for her on commission. If she wouldn't listen to that then I'd buy it for resale myself, borrowing the money from Ralph.

"Tonight," she said. "Say nineish. You know my address. I've got our old apartment back. Maybe that means something to you?"

"Okay. Nine. One more thing, Judy. Did you do the news last night?"

"Yes. Like always during the week."

"Did you have anything on the news about either a fire at the zoo or a part of the zoo being closed?"

"We had both," she said.

"Thanks, Judy." I hung up before she could maybe start mentioning some of the crazy things that once had taken place in our old apartment.

THERE WAS TIME before I was due at Judy's place. Thinking about seeing her again mainly made me nervous. I got out a diet cola and drank it slowly, thinking about Judy, thinking about me, but nothing I thought of was rewarding.

I remembered something and tried once more to call Ray Washam, the lawyer who'd officiated at my disciplinary proceedings and thereafter, perhaps because he had to, recommended my disbarment or suspension.

This time the phone rang twice and was picked up.

"Mr. Washam?"

"Yes."

"This is Al Sears. Do you remember me?"

"I remember you, Al," he answered amiably. "You sound different."

"I've stopped drinking," I said. "I've not had a drink for a lot of months."

"That's good news," he said.

"I have a job now outside the legal field," I said. "What I called you about was the hearing."

"I can't advise you about changing the results there, Al."

"I understand that. I'm not trying to change things. But you heard the evidence against me and listened to the witnesses who testified. Did anything you heard sound fabricated or false?"

He was silent for a long moment. "I'm not sure. Someone

who acts as a judge never is. You know the old tale about trials. There's what actually happened, what the jury hears, and what the jury believes. Some of what was said was harsh, but there seemed sound basis in fact for the various complaints against you. They were that you were drinking and not paying attention to business. People you'd represented in criminal trials attempted to show they weren't guilty and that what you did to them in court caused them to be found guilty, but I didn't believe any of that. You were just drunk. Even drunk you were decent in court when you managed to be there. Sometimes you were late. Other times you didn't show at all. None of that really had a lot to do with the guilt or innocence of your clients."

"That was the way it was," I admitted. "Was there anyone, any witness, anyone you saw or heard about, who seemed personally angry enough at me to want revenge?"

"Not that I remember. Why ask that?"

"Someone wants it now," I said.

"Tell me about it."

I told him as briefly as I could.

"My Lord," he said when I was finished. "And you've quit drinking altogether?"

"Yes."

"I'm truly glad for you. And I wish there was something I could say that would help."

"What you've told me does help. It saves me checking possibilities that don't exist. Besides, I wanted to thank you for trying to be of help before and during the hearing. I think some of the things you said to me privately helped me in getting dry."

"If you stay that way you'll have a future again in the practice, Al. Call me when you get reinstated."

"I'll do that if I ever ask for reinstatement."

I hung up and stared at the phone.

I now was fairly sure that whoever was after me had to have come from a small, select crowd and not from the distant past.

And would I apply for reinstatement? Maybe yes. Maybe no. Maybe sometime. Maybe never.

13

Wednesday, July 24, 9:05 P.M.

THE PARKING LOT was, as it had almost always been, dark. For the rent charged, as I remembered, the corporate ownership could have provided decent lighting. It didn't. Perhaps because the apartments were mostly occupied by high-salaried youngish executives ownership maybe believed dark parking lots would appeal to the tenants.

Knowing the territory allowed me to thread my way around decorative rocks, bushes, and flower beds without stumbling over anything lethal. Light from windows helped, but someone unfamiliar with the layout could and, many times, had wound up in a bush on moonless nights like this one. I remembered claims and lawsuits that had obviously taught ownership nothing. There was a large, well-lighted visitors lot up front, but it had been full. That was because many tenants parked there.

I climbed steps to the second floor and knocked on a familiar door. It was opened immediately.

Framed in dim light behind her, Judy seemed more lovely than ever. She wore a fashionable pseudosweatsuit that would die of embarrassment if sweated in, plus a matching sweatband around her handsome head. The way the sweatsuit fitted, inner knowledge made clear to me there was nothing underneath. My pulse rate quickened.

She looked me over and invited me in.

"You look fine, Judy," I said.

"So do you."

Inside the light was brighter and crueler. She no longer looked as she'd once looked. She was carrying ten or fifteen extra pounds and there were tiny lines at her mouth and near her eyes I'd not seen before. She was still achingly lovely, but like me she'd gotten a little older. She'd lost her dewy look. Now pushing thirty, edge of never-never land. Time to figure your piece of the world out or make some concessions.

I'd been slumped, pudgy, and seedy in the last days of our marriage. Forsaking booze and cigarettes and watching what I ate and combining those with regular running and frequent work-outs had eliminated my problems. She measured what she saw with approval.

"Have a drink with me?"

I shook my head.

"I didn't mean alcoholic. Coffee?"

"Black, no sugar."

"I remember."

Toward the end of our time it had been black, no sugar, and lots of rum. She turned away toward the kitchen. I found myself watching interesting movements. Sex had been a part of our marriage that had been world class. Before drinking had finally destroyed desire, almost every meeting where we were alone had ended in bed. Judy had liked all of it.

Not a lot had changed in the apartment. I sat on the front edge of a chair I remembered and looked around, fighting nostalgia. I waited for Judy to return with the coffee. The oversize television was off for once. I couldn't remember it being off much of our time, even when we were making love back then. Judy was a television omnivore.

She returned in moments. She bore a large, steaming mug in

each hand. Mine was straight coffee, midnight black and strong. I could tell from the aroma she'd tipped something extra into hers, probably Jameson's Irish. That had been her drink, seldom to excess, except on nights when she had the whole next day off. Even when she drank too much on those nights she'd always been able to throw off the effects of alcohol. She was healthy and made for children, but the idea of having a child horrified her.

I took a sip of coffee and put my mug on a small table near my side. Judy settled into a couch opposite my chair. She held her cup in front of her face with both hands and watched me over the rim.

"I'm going to get married again, Al," she said.

"You'll always be wed to a television screen, Judy," I said, smiling. It was something I'd at first kidded her about, then later became jealous of. I'd become jealous of a lot of things before heavy drinking removed those burdens.

She smiled her perfect white smile. "I really am getting married again."

"I know. To Robbins Whitehead. I talked with him at his office. Didn't he tell you?"

She shook her head and I could read her eyes. I figured Robbins would catch it up the line. Judy didn't like secrets she wasn't privy to. "Does it bother you I'm getting married again?" she asked, recapturing control of our conversation.

"Sure. I'm jealous, but we're divorced. I wish you better luck this time around."

She leaned forward and I saw she'd unzipped the top of her sweatsuit some more. Enough for me to glimpse old friends. I picked up my coffee cup and hid inside it.

"Aren't you curious about why I'm marrying Robbins, Al?"

I put my cup on the table. "It's none of my business."

"Damn it all, Al, it's your business more than anyone's. We loved each other. Once, we were married." She put her own mug down hard and got to her feet. Her breasts jutted out and she wore a frown. It was the Judy I knew best and sometimes wanted to forget. She was beautiful, but she also was in control of her life. She took what she wanted and left behind, in ruins, what she didn't.

Without consciously willing myself to do it I rose to my feet and crossed the small stretch of thick carpet that separated us. That brought a smile and a glint of triumph to her eyes. We were in each other's arms. She sank back on the couch, pulling me with her, making little animal sounds in her throat. She whispered old, remembered words in my ear.

I'm unsure what stopped me. Maybe it was the taste of Irish whiskey in her mouth, but I'd tasted second-hand booze before. Maybe it was pride, something akin to the same thing that had made me stop drinking. I wanted Judy, but I didn't want her to decide exactly what my future was to be with her. If we were about to make love then I wanted input into when, where, why, and how.

"All right, tell me why you're marrying Robbins?" I asked from an inch away.

"Why not? He's a great front for a working news girl." She looked into my eyes. "Can someone like Robbins keep you and me apart?"

"I hear you've also discovered a liking for my old friend and client, Duke."

"We snuck out once or twice," she said, grinning impishly.

"I thought you hated him?"

"I did when I had you." She smiled. "Forget Robbins and Duke. Let's take tonight. I want you and I know you want me. I want what we had together. You and I are adults. Robbins isn't here in this room. Duke's cute, but also crazy. He wants to be named king or something. Remember, I'm not remarried yet. There's not even that to stop us unless there are bad things the whiskey did you've not recovered from."

"I'm first class," I said. "Everything works fine, good as new. When I want it to work."

"It felt to me like that time was now." She waited.

"No, not now," I said, uncertainly. "I came to talk with you about your chain cent. That's why you called me, isn't it?"

She nodded, but when her voice came there was suppressed fury. "You always cared more about coins than about me."

"Not when we began."

I took two steps away and waited. She nodded again, making up her mind about something. She brushed abruptly past me and went to a writing desk in the corner of the room. She jerked open a door, pulled out a small velvet bag, and opened it. I saw the coin come out of the bag in its plastic holder. She hurled it at me in an athletic overhand. "Take the damned thing. Robbins will buy me a dozen of them if I ask. I don't want anything of yours around to remind me of you."

Her throw was wide, but I snagged the holder in my right hand as it flashed by.

"Go away," she said. "Leave."

"I won't take it. I'll buy it."

She lowered her head and got her temper back under control. "Whatever, Al. I swear I wouldn't have sold it to Harvey Kendall. I just wanted to see you." She came close to me and put out a hand that touched my wrist. She shivered a little. "What happened to all the good times, Al?"

"I don't know, Judy. I do know that I can't go back there again without a drink in my hand."

She stood there without speaking. She managed to put a tiny tear in each eye. I'd seen her do that on television at times. She was good.

I opened her door and let myself out.

I thought she'd regret me for a short time and then go on to planning on someone or something else. It was her way.

And yet . . .

IT WAS STILL muggy outside, but not as unpleasant as when I'd arrived. More apartment dwellers had turned off their lights and the parking area seemed black as pitch now that I'd exited the brilliant foyer.

I went down the steps that ended in the parking lot. I turned in the general direction of where I'd parked the VW. I heard, somewhere very near, a rustle and a grunt, as though someone in the darkness had tripped. It alarmed me and I spun to the right. A large form appeared dimly, almost unseen. The form held something upraised. I dropped to one knee and threw up my arms to protect myself. A moment later something smashed into my right forearm. I heard a snapping sound and knew that a bone was broken.

The pain was fierce. I'd have screamed, but I'd lost my breath. My large opponent crashed silently into me, flailing and kicking at me.

I huddled trying to protect my arm, but it became plain that more than my arm was planned to be involved.

The assailant kicked at my head, muttering gutter filth. I made out, in the darkness, his stepping away from me and saw his foot raised to stomp. I slammed upward at him, bringing him down. I wasted milliseconds trying to find the weapon he'd used on me.

I spotted something in loose marble chips. I reached for it as he rushed me again. I went into bushes, doubling the pain in my right arm. I swung my left fist as hard as I could as I was falling back. I heard a muffled curse and felt my fist impact his face.

We grappled blindly. I now could see and distinguish form, but nothing else. I thought I was done. I gasped for breath and the pain in my arm edged at my brain. I flailed away with my left arm in an effort to slow blows.

The door of a nearby apartment opened a crack, letting out a ray of light. A voice called: "Who's out there?"

My assailant ran into the darkness and away. I lay on the ground and let him go, fighting a tide that threatened to sweep me away.

I stayed conscious. I rolled off my arm and onto my back.

The voice from the apartment called, "Go away before I call police." The door slammed and the light vanished.

My assailant had fled. I couldn't hear anything of him now. I sat and carefully unfastened buttons on the front of my shirt, using the shirt as a makeshift sling. I was then able to get to my feet without passing out.

Once upright I searched the darkness until I found what I was looking for. It lay just off the sidewalk, under a bush. It was an old, weathered shovel, about four feet long from blade tip to handle end. *The weapon.*

I took it with me. I found my car and dropped the shovel in the back floor. I drove to Methodist Hospital on Union.

14

"WHAT YOU NEED to do is hire your own full-time private investigator to act as your bodyguard," Ralph said the following morning when I appeared. He locked the front door, put up the CLOSED sign, and listened carefully to what had happened. He put the chain cent in the safe. "It stays there until I work a deal for it."

"And get it approved by Judy," I added. "It's hers, not mine."

"Where was the gun you borrowed from me?"

"In my kitchen," I said lamely. "I didn't want to take a gun to Judy's." I'd put Ralph's gun next to Harlan's on a high shelf in the kitchen of my apartment.

Ralph shook his head in disbelief at my stupidity. "What did the police say?"

"Nothing, because I didn't call them. The doctor at the hospital wanted me to call them until I told him I fell down some steps."

"You should have called the police."

"I was with Smitty yesterday. They'd be interested if I could tell them who it was that attacked me. The snake thing puzzled Smitty. He's also puzzled about Benny and about who hired who."

All I had as a souvenir was the shovel that was used on me.

Early that morning, in the light, I'd found it had the name of Judy's apartment building stenciled on the handle.

"How about fingerprints? Did you think about that?"

"Not a hell of a lot. I think I have an idea who used the shovel. I'm going to do my own checking. I left a calling card on him. I'm going to check and see if I can find that calling card now."

He shook his head some more. "The way you look I can do without you being around today scaring customers. Tonight we set up for the show. Think you can help out some on that?"

"I can try," I said. "I don't believe the attack last night fits in with the other two."

"Who do you think it was?"

"I'm not dead certain yet, but I'll soon be and then I'll tell you. Last night's man wasn't professional and wasn't a planner. He was armed with a shovel he probably found in a flower bed. He dropped the shovel after his first good whack and tried to do the rest with his hands and feet. He was drinking and mad."

"Maybe the guy who put the snake in your car was drunk," Ralph said darkly. "The guy who came into the poker game with the shotgun was on drugs."

"Sure, but dropping the snake in my car has a sense to it of coolness and planning. The poker game got invaded by someone with a gun, someone who did his homework and knew things, knew you and me. The man last night was muttering crap and he was in a rage. He dropped the shovel after one good blow. You can beat someone to death with your hands, if you work at it long enough, but a weapon's a lot quicker. He dropped his and never tried hard to find it."

"Maybe he just never happened to find it."

"Then there's the booze," I continued.

"How drunk was he?"

"Reasonably well along. Since I quit drinking I smell almost everything and he had the odor of a heavy habit drinker. Kind of like meat eaters. I can smell when someone's a vegetarian. It's a sweeter odor. There was old and new booze on this guy's breath. We fought for a few minutes. He had the smell of some-one who'd been hard at the bottle for a long time." I thought for a moment longer. "I remember another smell to him, too. Cologne. *Canoe.* It's a brand I once wore myself. I gave it up. Judy liked it, though."

"You're sure who it was, aren't you?"

"Yeah. I'm sure. The only thing is I'm going to be dead sure."

"What are you going to do about it when you're dead sure?"

"I'm thinking on it."

AT NOON I waited near the door of Robbins Whitehead's office. I found a convenient alcove where I could watch without being noticed much. It was the recessed door to an office that was being remodeled. I stood inside the recessed part and waited. When someone came past I acted out the part of someone seeking entrance into the office, puzzled that the door was locked. No one questioned me.

Robbins Whitehead came out of his door at twenty past twelve, when I was about to give up. He came out carefully. I noted that his face was bruised purple and one eye was swollen almost shut. He walked like a careful man after a heart attack, a man fearing another seizure.

My right arm was in a cast, the ulna broken, my shield when I'd warded off the shovel. Seeing Robbins's face made the arm hurt less. Robbins must have had something very important to do in the office to have come in today. He was a mess.

I watched him drag down the hall. For a moment I thought about following and confronting him, but decided it would do little good. He'd either deny my accusations or maybe he'd admit them. I wasn't in any shape for another battle. He was a lot larger and had two good arms. I thought maybe I could make him run, but I wasn't sure. I'd save him for another day.

I had the shovel in my car.

Maybe I could leave the shovel for him today so he'd know I knew.

He'd followed me to Judy's place, or been watching when I came calling. Jealousy and booze had driven him to come after me when I emerged. I'd thought it was him when he'd managed to vanish through the parking lot without falling over something. Like me he knew the parking lot a little.

If men around Judy and Judy around men made him burn with jealousy, he was in for some bad years.

I waited and watched until he took the elevator. I then took another elevator down to the street.

I found his car in a nearby parking garage I walked through. It was a beautiful old black Porsche, the same one he'd owned when I'd been going with and later married Judy. I remembered how he'd bragged about the car and I knew that people who own great cars seldom sell or trade them.

It was cool and dark where the car was parked. A sign painted on the wall showed the spot belonged to Robbins Whitehead. Executive parking area, rented by the month or year, picked by Robbins to keep the car out of the hot, damaging sun.

I took a slim jim out of my pocket and probed for the Porsche's door lock after trying the doors. I used the slim jim sometimes in repossessions. The long thin blade had a flange at the bottom for catching locks. It snapped the door lock up and I opened the door.

I went to my own car, which I'd parked nearby in a vacant, but name marked spot, in violation of the garage rules. I got the shovel.

For a long moment, standing at the opened door of the Porsche, I considered destruction. I could do damage to something that Whitehead loved and make it a something that would never be the same to him, even when repaired. I could probably get away with it.

Looking at the car reminded me of looking at the chain cent. It was a beautiful, old, rare car, black and shiny. It had a personality of its own.

I had loved Judy once and I had known jealousy.

I put the shovel down gently in the driver's seat and relocked the front door. I left no note, but only the shovel.

I drove out of the garage after paying my ticket.

I smiled at the gate attendant.

"Have a nice day," she said, impressed with the smile.

"I'm trying hard."

I called Ralph. He'd not yet eaten. I inquired what he wanted for lunch, then stopped at a Burger King on the way back to the shop.

Once back I did tell him who'd broken my arm. I didn't tell him any more. There was no reason. Instead I sat and ate my cheese Whopper and smiled virtuously at the reflection of myself seen in the shop window.

I was tired of being pushed and not being able to push back, but I'd resisted paying back a mere Judy lover. Savaging the inside of Robbins's car wasn't going to find the people or person who wanted me dead.

Robbins would have his own reward. Judy.

I considered the thought that Robbins might have hired the earlier attackers, but I gave it up. He had no good reason unless he was then, as he was now, so hung up on Judy that he needed to kill all her former husbands and boyfriends.

One ex-husband, but *lots* of boyfriends.

Could that be?

I found I could work some that afternoon, but not a lot. Ralph was solicitous, and kept jumping up for every customer who entered. It annoyed me a little, but it was his shop. After a while I gave up trying to help and went back to my private investigator's cubbyhole. I napped there until closing time. I awoke somewhat refreshed. The nap had helped my aches and pains.

15

Thursday, July 25, 5:00 P.M.

GUARDS AND BOURSE staff workers opened the doors for coin
dealers at five o'clock. Ralph closed the coin shop early and we
got our portable display cases and lights and loaded them into
Ralph's old, reliable Checker. I followed him around the interstate to the exit that led to the huge Kaleidescope Hotel near the
river. There was room to park near the front of its convention
hall. We left Ralph's car and mine there while we hauled in the
coins and equipment.

Uniformed guards watched all. We drew identification badges
at the door and found our table by checking a map. The map
listed names of dealers and their tables by numbers. The names
and numbers were also posted above the tables so that a buyer
would have two ways of finding his way back for a wanted coin.

Other dealers were arriving. I saw Harlan Roberts talking to
uniformed and plainclothes special police at the entrance. I supposed his company held the security contract. He waved at us
and I waved back with my good arm. The broken arm ached, but
I could stand it.

Harlan approached. "Jesus, Al. What now?"

"Nothing. It's got nothing to do with the other stuff."

Harlan nodded and moved on.

Ralph was looking around from behind our table like a kid at a carnival. He'd even ignored Harlan.

"Go on out and cruise the floor," I said. "I'll set up the lights and put the coins in the cases."

"Can you do that with only one good arm?"

"If I can't I'll come after you."

"I'm off, then."

He left and I went through the business of setting up. I hooked clamps on the table and mounted adjustable lights to them. I hooked plugs into an extension cord and plugged into a hot line under our backup table. I opened boxes of coins in two-by-twos and put the coins neatly into the cases, lining them up by denominations and types. I saved space at the bottom of one case for a pile of type currency and Nationals that Harlan had already picked over. Some of the paper might be of interest to other buyers. The work was awkward for me, but using my right arm in its sling where I could, I managed.

Dealers came by looking. One examined large cents, but most of ours weren't much. I sold half a dozen medium-expensive Morgan dollars, the best of which was an 1894 in extra fine, to a New York City dealer. I sold some low-grade type coins to a New Orleans dealer I knew only by reputation and his ads in *Coin World*. Things slowed up after an hour. I stopped having a steady stream of seekers with want lists. A paper dealer from Ohio came by and bought some Nationals. He was followed by a man who did an auction list out of Louisville.

Ralph passed me by a few times, hurrying here, hurrying there. Eventually he came back and stopped.

"Close her down, Al. Lock the cases and cover up. Stick chairs on top. Then go to the table on the right of the far corner." He pointed. "They've got some nice copper I want you to look over."

I could tell he was still excited.

"When's it open in the morning?"

"Dealers at eight, public at ten."

"I've sold maybe five thousnad," I said, calculating in my head. "No checks to come. Everything written down and paid for."

Ralph nodded, smiling. "It's not the principal, Al. It's the interest." He walked away.

A bourse table closes when you turn off the lights and cover the cases up. I locked flimsy locks on the glass topped cases, covering the cases up with cloths furnished by either the show sponsors or the hotel, bent the lights down to the cloth after turning them off. I put the tilted chairs upside down over the lights. I wondered again, as at past coin shows, why anyone bothered to close up. Maybe a sheet, a chair, and a ten-cent lock would keep out a casual thief, but someone with determination would be through the defenses in five seconds. Sheets and no lights did alert security people you were closed, maybe allowing them to better watch anyone who lingered near a "closed" table.

I walked to the table Ralph had asked me to visit. It was still open. Ralph sat behind it in conversation with a heavily bearded man about his age. Both of them wore guns. Once again I'd left my pair in the apartment.

The man had one case full of large cents and half cents. There were two chains. The best one was a light-year from being as good as the one Judy had flung at me in her snit the night before. This dealer's probably graded very fine. The other was only very good. There were five 1793 wreath cents and an array of various tough dates. There were some early half cents, three of them 1793's. There was an 1802 in a higher grade than I'd ever seen. Maybe very fine plus.

Ralph and the owner watched me looking things over.

"Open the case," the owner said.

"No need. Looks nice from here and I'd only be looking and bothering."

Ralph grinned. "This is Al Sears. He works some for me in the shop when he's not investigating something. He used to practice law, but now he's a private detective. This is Honest Joe Hooker, Al. He specializes in early copper."

I remembered the name from coin paper ads.

"Al knows copper pretty well," Ralph continued. "He used to collect it and type coins."

Tucker nodded with interest. "Type *and* copper?"

"Yes. For a while."

Ralph said, "Al was once the owner of the Kaywenere Chain."

"What happened to it?" Hooker asked.

"My wife divorced me and took it in the settlement." I nodded at Ralph. "Ask Ralph about it rather than me."

"You got it now, Ralph?"

"Not yet and not for certain. Maybe."

Hooker turned back to me. "If your wife got the Kaywenere Chain in the divorce what did you get?"

"A long party and a lot of headaches." I looked into his case again, moving close to the glass. I'd built up a little money since I'd gone to work in Ralph's shop. I'd thought the urge to spend it on coins had abated, but in the presence of copper it had sprung back to life.

Tomorrow, first thing after a night of sleeping the urge off and hoping it'd not return, maybe I'd buy a piece of two from Hooker. The 1802 was likely out of my league, but maybe other things weren't. The 1802 was a tough date in half cents, more correctly described as an 1802 over 1800. I liked what I could see of it from the obverse.

There was also a 1799 large cent in passable condition, a difficult early date. I'd never owned one when I was collecting because I'd never seen one that satisfied me. This one wasn't high in grade, maybe fine, but the surface of the coin seemed nonporous.

"I've got authentication papers on the 1799," Hooker said.

"Let me take it and the 1802 half cent out," I said, overcome and therefore changing my mind.

"All right. I'll lift the case lid for you." He did and smiled at Ralph. "I'm glad you vouch for this man. I once had a guy with an arm sling who lifted two gold coins by sneaking them inside his cast."

I laid the two coins on the closed case. Hooker ignored me. I inspected the 1799 first. Up close I didn't like it as well as I'd liked it in the case. It had reverse rim damage that was distracting. I put it down and looked over the half cent. The reverse was better than the obverse, no porousness, no damage. It was the kind of coin that would stop any copper lover. Hooker's price was marked on it, high, but not out of reason. Most dealers will reduce sticker prices. We did. I wondered what Hooker would do if I asked in the morning.

Hooker saw I was done. He lifted the case lid and I replaced the two coins.

"Anything else?"

"I'll maybe talk to you about the half cent in the morning before things open."

"Okay," he said. "You want me to put it aside?"

The fever burned a little and I nodded. I could always tell him I'd come to my senses overnight and pass the coin by.

"There's some room in it. It came in a set I bought over the counter last week. I've never seen an 1802 that beats it, outside big-time auction lots."

I nodded and looked up at his name and table number wanting to make certain I remembered. His table was 31.

Something came to me.

I dug in my billfold and got out the numbers Benny Wilson had secreted under the blotter on his desk. Yes, there was a number 31 there. I looked around the room. One listed number I could see was 76. I'd thought that Benny maybe bet that number. Now 76 turned out to be the table of a dealer in Indiana, one who carried ten million plus in inventory, and traveled to shows in an armored bus. I could see his armed police officers, two of them, sitting at his backup table.

I counted fourteen numbers on Benny's list. One was Ralph's. Each number seemed to be that of a dealer with class merchandise. Some of the numbered dealers hadn't arrived yet, but would in the morning. Big dealers.

I got Ralph from behind Hooker's table. I led him to a quiet spot and told him about it.

"Maybe coincidence," he said uneasily. "Or maybe Benny saw

an advance list and wrote down the numbers of dealers he wanted to see."

"Possibly," I admitted. "Another guess would be that Benny obtained the dealer table numbers early and then sold them to someone who has plans for the show. Theft. Armed robbery. *Something.*"

Ralph shook his head. "Robbery would be hard. Look around, Al. This camp is armed. A sneak thief, maybe someone who dealt with Benny for the list, might steal something at a table when the crowd got heavy, but it'd take an army to stick up this place."

"It would by day. How about at night? Guys armed with machine pistols and dynamite. They could blow in a whole wall. And they'd be more heavily armed than Harlan's guards."

Ralph looked over the rows of bourse tables, most lights now off. "In a bit this room will clear. They'll lock the doors and half a dozen officers will stand guard until morning. I can't get back in, you can't. No one can."

"How about entry through dynamite?"

"I don't know. It'd have to be wired and set off. People in the motel would see and hear."

"But Harlan could get in, Ralph." I remembered the fine home complete with housekeeper. A lot of dollars for a black ex-cop. The snake had been dropped in my car there. And Harlan had been out of sight for a suspicious while. "How about Harlan setting a robbery up?"

"I've known him for years," Ralph said. "He was a damned good police officer. He now runs a money-making special police company. He married a lady whose father was one of the first black millionaires in Memphis. I've done my business with him by handshake for twenty years. I'd trust my life with him. Remember, one more time, that he killed the guy who tried to take us from my poker game."

"People who marry money and make money sometimes want lots more. Maybe he saved our asses because that was the thing to do," I said, refusing to give up.

145

"No, Al. You were tumbling that Shell guy and couldn't see it happen. I was scared, but I saw it all. Harlan went for his gun the instant you gave him an opening. No hesitation. You'd be dead now and maybe I'd also be dead if it hadn't been for Harlan."

"Duke had a gun," I said lamely.

"He'd have shot his toes off. He's a dreamer and a bumbler. He's so crazy he quit collecting coins about the time prices doubled. Maybe he's also into butterflies now."

I waited.

"Let's find Harlan and tell him what you've got."

We found Harlan.

16

Thursday, July 25, 9:45 P.M.

WHEN I MANAGED to get away from Harlan and the questions
he had for me after the closing of the coin show, there was still
one more thing I wanted to do. I drove the Dasher to Germantown again and on toward Abraham Burks's estate. On the way
I ran through one of those sudden, gullywasher thunderstorms
that plague Memphis in summer. It was ten minutes of fury and
fireworks, but it was all over and the skies were clearing when I
arrived at the road on which Abe lived.

From my earlier visit I knew that Abe's near-mansion sat close
to the road with at least thirty or forty acres surrounding the big
house. The driveway I'd driven down a few days back had been
bordered by carefully manicured lawns, precise plantings, and
shaded by fine old trees. Behind Abe's house there was first the
big pool, and then the lake, maybe fifteen acres of water, too large
to be called a mere pond. I'd not seen a lot of that lake during
my visit, but I had seen a dock, and a boat probably for fishing
use. I'd also noted that outdoor tables and chairs were scattered
in a cleared, well-trimmed area near the dock. On the far side of
the lake the trees were dense, with limbs hanging down near the
water surface in places.

Abe's place was on the far side of Germantown, away from

crowded business and the smaller residential districts. It was the kind of place that by size and value was a true "estate." He had neighbors, but those neighbors, like him, had distanced themselves from the rest of the world by surrounding themselves with insulating expanses. I thought the main things the residents of the rich area shared were desires for quiet and privacy.

I passed fancy mailboxes and several closed, locked gates as I got close to Abe's. The headlights of the car picked out a mailbox on a column of white bricks, surmounted by a foot-high miniature of a rearing white horse I'd noticed last time. I then knew that Abe's place would be next.

I slowed. The narrow, well-kept road I was on was hemmed in closely by both trees and fences on both sides, but when driving away from Abe's before I'd noticed a narrow gravel lane on the opposite side of the road, about a hundred yards from the gate that opened to Abe's estate.

I looked in my rear mirror. From a long way back I could see lights, but I had time.

The lane was hard to see at night. I almost drove past it before recognizing it. I hit the brakes, backed up a little, and then nosed the Dasher into it. I waited until the car that had been behind me drove slowly on past. Then I drove about a hundred or so feet up the lane before pulling off as far as I could against wild bushes at the side of the road.

From its unused appearance, I doubted that the road was anyone's path or driveway. I thought my car would be safe and undisturbed for as long as I wanted to leave it.

I opened my glove compartment and took out a set of 7×50 binoculars that I'd purchased several years earlier just before attending my one and only greyhound race across the river in West Memphis, Arkansas. Once at those races was enough. Watching a pack of emaciated dogs chase a mechanical rabbit hadn't held a lot of appeal for me, so I'd never gone back. Besides bar service had been poor and the drinks heavily watered. I'd put the binoculars in the glove compartment and forgotten them until recently. I was surprised they'd lasted in the glove compartment this long, thieves being what they are and my attention to safely locking doors being what it was.

I also got out a penlight. The batteries were weak, but a small ray of light came from it when I turned on the switch.

The night was dark, but the sky had clear spots. The moon had not yet risen. I had no idea what good the binoculars would be, but decided it was better to have them and not need them than need them and not have them. I slipped the leather strap over my neck. I got out and locked the car.

I walked back to the main road and then, keeping poised to leap for cover should I see or hear any sign of traffic on the road, I resumed my journey on foot.

A dog became aware of me when I was about fifty yards from the entrance to Abe's estate. He barked for a while. I crossed the road, ignoring him, and found a sheltered place behind a tree near Burks's entrance. I watched.

I waited patiently for a long time, but nothing of note happened. A man with a leashed Doberman passed along the fence. I didn't know whether it was the same one I'd seen before, in the daytime, or a new one.

No one entered or exited Abe's gate.

If he was involved in my present situation, the fact that nothing was happening at his entrance made no difference. He could have done any business he needed by phone or by sending a message out with Lefty hours or days ago.

Down the road, away from Abe Burks's entrance, around a long curve, was the place I'd met Millie a time or two when she'd sneaked outside the fence. I walked that way. I found, or believed I found, the place where she'd exited and met me in the past. I examined the fence in that area with the penlight, but if there was an opening now I couldn't locate it. Maybe Abe, after Millie had vanished with her gold, had found this chink in his defenses and closed it. There was nothing now to indicate that there'd been an opening in the fence.

I walked back to where I'd been. I watched for a while longer. I gave it up after about an hour and a half, during which the man and his Doberman had come past twice more at intervals of roughly forty-five minutes. Each time the pair had approached on my left and departed to my right, so I believed they were walking guard duty around a regular circuit within Abe's grounds. After giving the patrollers a few minutes to put distance between us, I got to my feet and headed back to my car.

I wasn't far from the lane where I'd hidden the car when I saw the tree. The thunderstorm I'd driven through had been brief, but in its short, savage life it had managed to do damage. There, in the dim starlight, I could see, fifteen feet up the side of one of the big trees growing just inside the barbed fence, the white scar left when a lightning bolt or gust of wind had ripped a huge limb half loose from the tree trunk. I'd not seen the downed limb on my way in because it had been away from where I'd walked and my eyes had probably not been as accustomed to the night. But now, after an hour of darkness plus, I was coming upon it from the opposite direction, and my eyes, now night adjusted, showed what had happened.

I pushed my way through the foliage. I grasped the huge limb with my good arm and tried to shake it. It didn't budge. Although its massive weight had crashed it to the ground it still seemed securely fastened to the bole inside the fence. At light tomorrow, Abe or one of his employees would discover what had happened. The limb would be quickly cleared away, but at this moment I hoped I was the only one who knew that Abe's fancy fence had been breached by nature.

It seemed an omen. I didn't believe in that sort of thing, but still it seemed as though some force had arranged the storm for my benefit. The broken limb would be a cinch for me to climb, even with one of my arms in a sling. Maybe I could find an easy way down across the fence. I put a foot on the branch and began to ascend.

The fallen limb had not damaged or even touched Abe's fence. I climbed well above it on my way to the tree inside the barrier. Once there, I found it possible to descend to the ground by way of other limbs that ended about waist high from the ground.

Once down on the ground and inside Abe's estate, I stopped to think about what to do. So far I'd acted on impulse and that could end up being dangerous. I had no particular reason other than curiosity and fear for coming out and watching Abe's place this night. I had had no intention of entering it, but now the opportunity had come and I wanted to take advantage of it. I'd come to watch because that was a part of what I was. Someone wanted to kill me, someone watched and waited. It was possible that person or persons were Abe's hired men.

I knew I didn't have long. The man-dog patrol had gone past perhaps five or six minutes earlier, which meant I had about forty minutes before it returned. I didn't know much about dogs, but I feared the Doberman would be able to tell that I'd been there. As soon as he passed this spot again he'd set up a ruckus, and if I was still inside I'd be in trouble whichever way the dog ran. So, if I ventured a mission it needed to be a short one. I looked at my watch. Ten minutes short of midnight. I was taking a chance by assuming that the patrol made one circuit every forty-five minutes like clockwork. I'd only had a few circuits to base my conclusion on. I thought about it for a moment and decided to take the risk. I'd give myself some leeway. Ten minutes. That meant I had a half an hour to see what could be seen, then I had to be back at the tree, over it, and off Abe's property.

I looked around for some landmark by which I could find my way back to my tree, the downed branch being only seeable once you were near it. There was a bush shaped like a mushroom about sixty feet out and off to the left. When I couldn't see anything else like it I decided it would have to do. I struck out toward the house. I was away from the lakeside here and my easiest approach was toward the left wing of the house, now completely dark.

City dwellers like to think the country is quiet. It wasn't on this night. I made my way across close-mown grass. I heard loud chirps and cries of insects and, far from me, at the lake, the assertive peeps and croaks of frogs. Night birds fluttered in trees I passed and called out to each other. I added as little noise as possible to the racket.

I arrived at the side of the house a little out of breath from tension and exertion. I looked at my watch and saw that five of my minutes had elapsed. I looked into each of the windows that were available on that side of the house, but I saw nothing. The windows were heavily curtained. I backed up a few steps and looked up at the second-floor windows. Not a pinpoint of light showed.

I moved around the corner to the front of the house.

There was nothing there, either. I walked carefully across the front drive of the house, checking the windows. Again, no light showed through, but I did observe a faint glow in the fanlight above the big front door. It could mean a light in the central hallway or perhaps just a nightlight in some room with its door left ajar.

I continued looking along the far side of the house with the same results. It wasn't until I got to the back of the house, the lakeside, that I could see any evidence that the house wasn't deserted on this night. One window on the second floor showed a mild glow, as if it might be given off by a bedlamp. Two downstairs windows spilled bright rectangles on light out onto the piazza I stood on. The big expanse of windows I'd passed in my earlier visit were now curtained over.

I made my way stealthily to the nearest of the bright windows and peeked in, exposing only an eye and part of my face. I was looking into a huge kitchen. At a table near its center sat Abe's man Lefty, one big hand wrapped around a beer bottle and the other holding a copy of *Playboy*. As I watched he sat the bottle down and dug into an opened can of dry roasted peanuts. He tossed them in his mouth, and looked up toward my window. I thought he might see me, but I also thought it was safer to leave my head where it was than to move it.

He looked back down and resumed his grip on the beer bottle without any sign of alarm. Maybe he was interested in the foldout in *Playboy*. He turned a page and leaned back. I could see he carried a gun stuck inside his waistband. If he saw or heard me I could very easily get my butt shot off.

From what I could see he was alone in the kitchen. I ducked down and made my way past the closed back door to the other illuminated window. It also opened into the kitchen and a quick glance told me he was alone.

I abandoned him to the centerfold and stood there for a few moments considering the situation. Lefty was there in the kitchen. Perhaps he'd left the upstairs light on, or there was someone else up there in that lighted room. It seemed possible to me that the upper room was Abe's bedroom and Abe was in it.

That speculation, even if true, didn't mean a lot to me. My time was running out—my watch now showed five minutes past. I didn't have time to wait until Lefty finished his snack and magazine and went finally to bed. Even if I had all night I'd found nothing to stay for. I wasn't going to break in with a guard inside and a guard with dog outside. I had nothing to look for.

I stood there feeling stupid. I realized again I was watching people just to see what was happening. I'd done it with Duke and I'd done it with Ace and Deuce. I'd learned little.

Spying inside here was stupid.

I headed back toward the fence, this time dropping near the lake to take advantage of cover seen down the sloped lawn near the shore. I'd moved to within fifty feet of the water's edge when it happened.

There was a faint, harsh sound from the direction of the lake. I stopped and at that instant caught a glimpse of a flash of light out of the corner of my left eye. For a split second I thought someone had fired a gun at me, perhaps from on around the lake. Then I realized, as a bead of sweat rolled down my back, that it wasn't so. The noise and the light had come from the dock-deck, not from on around the lake. Someone had flicked a cigarette lighter. In my concentration on the house I'd forgotten the dock on the lake. Someone was there now, maybe looking directly at me, perhaps sighting me in down the barrel of a gun. I shivered in the muggy air, I wanted to run, but I was frozen. The night around me smelled of decaying vegetation and my sweat.

I crouched and stayed unmoving. There was no further movement or noise from the dock. Someone was sitting or standing there. Someone had been there all the time I snooped the house.

I thought it was possible that the person there had not seen me, might be as ignorant of my presence as I'd been of his until he lit his cigarette. I could now see a tiny red light from that cigarette. That light remained in the same spot.

I'd been careful, but anyone watching the house could have seen my head silhouetted against the kitchen windows while I was looking in. But if I'd been seen there'd have been an outcry and an alarm. Besides the person on the dock wouldn't have alerted me to his presence by lighting a cigarette while I was around. I decided he'd been looking over the lake during crucial moments. He must have been, for it was now apparent he'd not seen me.

I slowly let myself sink to the ground, keeping myself in a position where I was looking at the dock area. I looked hard, but those glimpses into the bright occupied kitchen had temporarily destroyed most of my night vision and I could make out nothing but vague shapes and the glow of the cigarette tip. I hoped that the night vision of whoever was out there, and I thought it was Abe Burks, had been damaged just as much or more than mine by the flare of the lighter.

I couldn't stay here forever. I looked at my watch again; 12:08. Twelve minutes left of my self-imposed deadline.

I huddled on the ground. I wasted my energy trying to will the man to go back into the house so that I could get away. I could now see the glow of the cigarette tip and the outline of the man smoking it rather than only imagine him. Night vision was returning.

I saw a glowing arc float through the air and thought I heard the faint hiss as the cigarette was extinguished in the lake.

The man I was watching arose from somewhere on the dock

and walked across to the railing farthest from the shore. He stood there for a long moment, looking out into the lake.

He said something softly to the water. I listened, trying to make it out, but I was unsure. *Was it "Millie?"*

It was Abe Burks. I was now sure of that.

I continued to watch. Something out there in the water or under the water interested him.

Is that where Millie is, Abe?

No, they drug the lake.

I watched while the man walked slowly off the dock and back up to the house. I confirmed my guess when the door opened and the light revealed Abe Burks wearing a robe and pajamas. The door closed behind him and I was once more alone.

My watch now read 12:22, two minutes past my deadline, and I needed to get swiftly back to the fence. Almost all of my night vision had returned and I was covering now familiar territory. I set out toward the fence at a quick trot. It was awkward going with my arm in a sling.

I found the mushroom bush without difficulty, but then I wasted minutes trying to figure out which tree it was I'd come over the fence on. The scar, visible from the road, was hidden by night from sight on this side and all the big trees looked the same to me.

I was still searching when I heard the dog-man team approaching. In desperation, I got up into the nearest tree and climbed up ten feet, pulling myself awkwardly up by one arm. As soon as I was that high I could see a bit of the white scar up the trunk of the next tree over. There was now no way I could get over to that tree without going back down my tree to the ground. It was too late to do that because I could see and hear the dog. He was now in sight on the ground near my perch, whimpering excitedly at the strange and unexpected scent of me.

The guard had unleashed the dog and was now urging him to violence with cries of "Attaboy, Toben! Sic 'em!" I hugged my tree trunk silently, waiting to be caught, hoping not to be shot.

The Doberman suddenly took off at a nose-to-ground run toward the house where I'd left a double scent, coming and going.

His human teammate followed close behind, gun at ready, hot for action.

As soon as they were a safe distance away, I dropped down from my perch, ran to the next tree, and climbed up and over to safety.

When I was on the ground on the outside of the fence my legs nearly gave way beneath me. I walked unsteadily across the road to the gravel lane and went down it as fast as I could manage.

It had been a very close thing.

I smiled a small smile of relief and fished for the keys to my car.

Someone whacked me solidly on the head as I tried to fit a key into the door. There was one quick flash of pain and brightness and then the dark closed all around me.

17

I CAME UP and out of darkness as they were pulling me from my car. The space I was in on the back floor of the Dasher was cramped. They had difficulty extricating me from between the seats. I stayed inert. I was aware enough to know it was *my* car I was in. They'd driven it and me someplace. The night sounds were different than they'd been on the road in Germantown. I could hear city and river sounds.

I came back to immediate full consciousness. There was none of the sluggishness that had followed the attack outside Judy's apartment. This time the switch flipped back on and the equipment in my head came on with it. All at once. I hurt, but I was accustomed to hurting by now.

"Heavy bastard," one of them said in a voice I thought I recognized. Someplace I'd heard the voice before.

"I don't know why we didn't finish him off where we slugged him," said another voice querulously. "I know the boss says this one needs to look like an accident, but how fancy does it have to be? We could of stuck the hose we bought onto his exhaust pipe and run it in a window. Or we could have made it look like a robbery, like the other one. The cops think it was a mugging, from what's been in the papers."

"We're going to do it like the man planned, Micko," the familiar voice answered. "The boss seen this place and he showed it to me. It's deserted and stays that way. No damn cops or kids. We're going to let him kill himself neat, clean, and clever. No one will believe it's any other way. I remember him when he was my lawyer. And I remember seeing him falling around on the street. He's a born-again drunk. He's going to fall a long way off his alky-wagon."

"Yeah, yeah," the one called Micko answered. "You and the man had big ideas about how that snake was going to do for him, too."

"That's crap. We still are trying to figure how he got out of his car alive. I read the stuff on the zoo sign. That snake was poisonous. I was glad to drop it out of the burlap and get away from there. Damn snakes make me sweat." He went on with assurance. "But no problem. He won't get out of this alive. I double-damn well guarantee it."

"He better not," Micko said, laughing a little. "The man will commit suicide himself if this guy gets away again. He's had cat's lives." His voice took on a slightly pleading note. "Look, let me finish him off now and we'll get out of here. A couple more good taps on the head and he'll sleep forever. Then we could go drink a beer or three."

I tried opening my eyes a little. It was dark and all I could make out were forms and a little movement.

"No way. I owe this guy a thing or two. I want him to see and know what's coming. Put your sap away." He laughed and I could see him, out of eyes opened only to slits, poke the other jocularly in the darkness. "Stick with me. I'll learn you how to take pride in your work. So go and get the sack of stuff out of the car. Then stand back, with your sap in your back pocket, and watch. You'll learn from a true expert. And you'll maybe have some fun."

I heard Micko's footsteps crunch across rough ground. I decided it might be a good time to make a move. From what I'd heard unpleasant things were planned for me and I wasn't supposed to live though them. If I was going to spoil things then I'd have a better chance doing it while Micko was fetching the sack, even if that was only from a few yards away. I opened my eyes wide in the darkness so as to better assess the situation.

My watcher picked that moment to flick on his flashlight and it was pointed straight at my face. There was no use in pretending further, so I raised my good arm to shield my eyes.

"Welcome back, Al Sears. We've been hoping you would join the party with us," the voice said with false cheeriness. "You slept well for a reformed drunk. Pretty soon I'll give you your long sleep. You won't get a chance to mess up any more of my trials."

Although I still couldn't see the face I now remembered who the voice belonged to: Denzil Edward Chavez.

In the years I'd done criminal work I'd represented many people. Only a few had ever worried me and made me doubt the wisdom of accepting big money from them to defend them. My captor was one of those few. I'd represented him first at an early stage in my career. I'd represented him last maybe six months before the disciplinary hammer had fallen on me.

He was better known as "Sandman," or, for those he worked with, sometimes as "Sandy."

He was a viciously clever man. He hated well and planned well. He did a lot of things for a lot of bad people. He liked to inflict pain and liked also to play with his victims. I'd represented him first when his girlfriend had been found in the driver's seat of her car twenty feet deep in the river. She'd been tortured and tied tight to the steering wheel and then pushed, alive, into the river. The prosecution had, for evidence, Sandman's public threats, one beating inflicted, a hospital stay for the deceased girl recovering from that beating, and little else.

I'd mincemeated the prosecution in that one, winning a quick acquittal and the then approval of Sandman.

In the twilight of my legal career, when I was deep in drink, he'd not been so lucky. He'd been caught in a stolen car when he was on some kind of job. He never used his own vehicles when he was on his way to commit various felonies. Most of the felonies he'd been involved in had to do with human life, and so he would steal a car for coming and going. I'd thought, when I defended him that last time, that an alert traffic officer with a hot sheet had likely saved an unknown citizen's life.

Sandman was medium size, more than medium smart, and as amoral as a cat. He was a workout athlete, a lifter of weights, and a long-distance runner. He loved to punish victims for his master and for himself. He was, I now remembered, widely used in other cities, flown in and flown out after quick jobs. He got big money for those jobs. I remembered that I'd charged him tens of thousands of dollars for my last defense.

He'd grinned and paid up front, saying, "That ain't much."

I'd never heard of a Micko.

"I got a drink for you, Sears," Sandman said mockingly.

I didn't answer.

"What's wrong, Sears? You feeling antisocial?" The light stayed on my face, but I could tell from the sound of his voice that he'd turned his head.

He called, "Hurry on with that stuff, Micko. Friend Sears is awake. All of us are going to have a drink, like the good pals we are. Maybe we'll even have two drinks." He laughed a little, watching me in the light, maybe liking what he saw on my face.

"Not me, Sandy."

"Ah. I'm happy to see you recognize me, old pal. Remember how much good you did me that last time in court? I do. I remember it well."

"I suppose I could have had the traffic cop who stopped and arrested you murdered. I told you then you were lucky you got caught going someplace rather than returning from the scene of a crime. You got minimum sentence, Sandy. The cops were interested in some of the things that were in the car trunk, but I kept them out of evidence."

"You were drunk in court," he said, scandalized. "I could smell it on you. You slurred your words. The judge hated me because of you. So now we'll have a few snorts to celebrate that time. I know you can still handle it. Just like then."

Micko had returned. The light of the flashlight had closed my pupils down so that I could see little except the bright spot, but I could tell from the noises that Micko had returned with a sack of something.

The two rummaged through the sack, but the light didn't leave me.

"Here it is," Sandy said, seemingly delighted. "Sit up, Al."

I did so. I crossed my legs to fight dizziness. I leaned back against the side of my car. He tossed a pint of a cheap blended whiskey into my lap.

"It ain't the good stuff you were on during my trial, Al. But I hear you went down from there. I hear you got to the place where you drank everything all the way down to dollar wine. So uncap and have a shot. Now!"

I looked down at the bottle. I had drunk anything toward the end of my bad times. Scotch, bourbon, gin, vodka—anything with alcohol in it. Beer and wine, when the hard stuff wasn't available.

Sandman's blended brand wasn't the worst I'd drunk, though it was years from the best. I looked at the bottle and found myself thinking that I'd *have* to drink it. In the months since I'd quit I'd had a thousand opportunities to drink and had answered "no" each time. It had been up to me whether I drank or not. I'd had the power to decline. And I had declined. I'd said no when I'd wanted to say yes—many times—but I'd always said no. Now I wasn't being asked, I was being told.

It's out of your hands, said a part of my brain. *This time you have no choice but to take a drink. And you want one. Oh, how you want and need one.*

"Get that cap off and drink up," Sandman said, impatience edging his voice. I heard a rough metallic sound. Someone had cocked a pistol.

Moving without me willing it, my left hand reached for and caressed the bottle. *My old flame.* There was an almost sensuous feel to the ribbed plastic cap, the rough paper of the tax stamp, and the cool, known smoothness of the glass bottle. Inside me, conflicting emotions warred. I wanted a drink. I was scared, but

I wanted a drink now, a place to hide. A smaller part of me shrank from the idea, fearful of what taking a drink could mean. Even with the likelihood of death only a few minutes away, that part of me still fought the prospect. The two parts struggled as I sat motionless, holding the bottle in my good hand.

"You want to get gut shot?" Sandman asked.

I waited. I doubted he'd shoot me. That was too easy and could have been done without all this.

"Micko," Sandman said, all playfulness vanished, "help Sears have a drink so he can join our party."

Before I could prepare at all, Micko brought his sap down viciously on the point of my good shoulder. I sucked in my breath and jerked my head back, banging it against the side of my car so hard that I almost lost consciousness.

I watched shooting stars. I hurt and my head buzzed.

"Drink now, Sears," Sandman said.

I sat straight again and now my shoulder ached in company with the arm that throbbed inside its cast. I placed the bottle between my knees. With my left hand I twisted off the cap and tossed it aside. The scent of the raw whiskey assaulted my nostrils immediately. The larger, dark part of my insides rejoiced. Hands trembling, I took the bottle from between my knees and raised it so that I could look within. I was going to die. Why not die as I'd lived? Booze had almost killed me. Now let it ease my way.

I lifted the bottle to an inch away from my mouth. The fumes invaded my nostrils. I had to swallow to avoid choking.

I tightened my hand around the bottle and then, with a sob that mourned the loss of booze and all the rest, I hurled the bottle savagely at Sandman.

I heard a satisfying clink as the bottle hit him somewhere, then Micko's sap put me down again.

I HURT ALL over when I came awake. My head ached, the shoulder of my good arm burned, my broken arm throbbed with pain, and my throat had a raw, scraped feel. There was a mix in with the bad of a few good things. I had a feeling of warmth in my stomach and that slowly was spreading outward, numbing the hurtful things. I sensed that soon my head, arm, shoulder, and throat would feel no pain at all.

I opened my eyes reluctantly. At first I thought that Sandman was still shining me with his flashlight. Then I realized I was looking up at the risen full moon. I reached my left arm out to steady me so that I could get to my feet. I touched nothing. There was still feeling in my hand, but there was nothing where I'd reached for my hand to touch upon.

I turned my head away from the moon to do eye exploration of my surroundings. My heart almost stopped at what I saw. I was lying on a ledge, roughly two feet wide by eight feet long, a long and high way up on the inside of a ruined building. Above me the roof was gone and all the floors above and below had collapsed, leaving behind an empty shell perhaps eighty to a hundred feet tall. The inside walls were interrupted here and there by remnants of floors, like the one I lay on. There were also occasional projections of reinforcing metal rods that had been used during long-ago construction to strengthen the floors.

I lay quietly. I thought it possible that Sandman and Micko were still someplace around and had left me only for a moment.

Just behind me was a door. I struggled to a sitting position and put my back against it, holding my legs sideways and keeping them on the remainder of the ledge. I then reached around and attempted to turn the door handle with my left hand. The handle turned easily and squeaked with the turns, but the heavy door didn't move when I tried to pull it toward me.

A voice inside me told me not to worry about minor problems. The warmth that was spreading upward from my stomach told me everything was all right. Just relax. Close your eyes again. Rest.

The temptation was almost overwhelming.

I leaned slightly forward. I put my head over the ledge, thrust two fingers of my left hand as deeply as I could into my throat, and pressed down on my tongue. I retched. That went on and on without interruption until I sat back against the door again, swallowing hard, stomach muscles still cramped with pain.

I knew by then that Sandman and Micko were gone. In my imagination I could hear Sandman laughing at me. He'd used his ideas on finesse well. When I'd thrown the bottle at him he'd taken another or others and poured booze down me after I was unconscious. The soreness in my throat was probably from a tube he'd used to make sure that the drink went directly to my stomach. From the amount I'd retched up he must have put a liter or two into me, taking no chances. If I'd continued to sleep maybe I'd have died of alcohol poisoning or one of the dozen other ways that alcohol, in quantity, can kill by stopping heart and brain. That was if I didn't fall off the ledge first and die in the rubble below. No matter. I could see Sandman smiling. I was dead. He'd hated me too bad to allow Micko to throw me off. He'd played with me as he'd mercilessly played with others. *Die in fear.*

I called out as loudly as I could. I called and called. No one came. The night around me remained as it had been. I could hear faraway train sounds and, now and then, I could hear big trucks on a distant roadway. Where I was I realized that there was no possibility that anyone would find and rescue me. Someday someone would find what was left. Long dead.

I thought I vaguely knew the place. In the nineteenth century, when Memphis was a booming river town sustained by cotton and other commerce, the floodplain bluffs of the river were lined with multistory buildings that housed small offices, warehouses, and manufacturing establishments. With the passage of years, most of those structures declined and were abandoned for newer buildings elsewhere in the city. Nature slowly reclaimed what had been abandoned. The long stretch of buildings had become an eyesore and a public nuisance. Within the past few years a few of the old structures, far away from this one, had been refurbished and put back into use again, but the rest were gradually being torn down. I'd read where the money had run out and more destruction had been delayed until next summer.

I listened to a fog horn on a river barge and knew I was trapped in one of the buildings marked for destruction—next year. I thought it was newer because of the steel that had obviously gone into its construction.

I remembered reading more about the renewal in the paper. A month or so back two kids had gotten into the project and been killed. The bodies had been found only after a long search. Now the buildings were posted and fenced. The paper had referred to the spot as the most deserted area in a hundred miles of river.

I sat there, back to the door, for a time, waiting to see what effect the alcohol I'd absorbed would have on me. I couldn't have been unconscious too long. All I felt was a mild buzz, akin to what I'd once gotten after a couple of morning screwdrivers or double-jolt Bloodies. There was none of the sluggishness that comes from high levels of alcohol in the blood. I thought it was even possible that the unaccustomed alcohol had shocked me back into consciousness.

I sat thinking in the moonlight. I was filthy and I reeked of booze kept and booze unkept. I felt the old, known effects of the liquor and I knew, with minor triumph, that I no longer wanted to drink. I didn't promise myself that if I got out of this I'd not drink again. There was no need. I just knew that all desire was now gone and the dark part that had existed inside me was stone dead. I didn't know exactly why it had died, but I knew it was so.

The moon had moved perceptibly by the time I came out of my reverie.

The far wall of the building was in black shadow, but the wall I was on was illuminated by bright moonlight. My eyes had accommodated themselves to the light. I could see nearly as well as on a heavily overcast day at sunset.

I could figure why Sandman and Micko had chosen this particular ledge. The wall below was virtually smooth, with no noticeable projections, and the remains of the floor, of which my ledge was the main remaining part, had crumbled away to almost nothing. There were a few odd projections here and there that might provide a foothold, but they were so widely and erratically spaced that they seemed worthless to me.

I could see that other walls below had windows and door openings, but the door at my back was the only opening on the floor of my wall. I turned to the door and tugged at the handle again, moving it this way and then that, but the heavy door remained firmly closed. There was no lock opening. Somehow they'd stripped the door before leaving me inside. If there were hinges they were on the other side of the door. I banged the door a few times hopefully. There was no effect except that a little of my ledge crumbled off by the door. The sound of its falling was frightening. I stopped my assault on the door.

I couldn't go down, and I couldn't go to either side. All that was left, unless I wanted to stay or fall from my tiny ledge, was to go up. I looked upward and didn't see how I could manage that, either.

The roof hadn't caved in as a single, coherent piece. Instead it had come apart slowly and fallen to the ground piece by piece, probably down through long years. Now there was little of it left, just patches of rubble suspended precariously at each of the four corners and a thick single metal beam that ran from the top of my wall across the open expanse to the top of the wall opposite.

That single beam adjoined my wall about ten feet above my ledge and away from it another twelve feet. It went up a good twenty feet to a point above it near where the ceiling had once been. I dismissed it at first because the distances were too great. The difficulty of getting to the beam seemed even greater than getting to the top of the remaining wall directly above me.

I sat again and examined and exhausted possibilities. If I waited then soon the sun would rise. It would dry me out, burn me up, and eventually I'd die. It might take days. I could dive down and make it swift.

I looked through my pockets for a pen or pencil. If I did die

I'd leave a note about Sandman and Micko. No pen, no paper. I did have the key to my VW. I could write on the wall.

I tried that. The old wall was hard as steel. I scratched and bent and looked, reading nothing. Besides, when I was dead, who'd check? A drunk had gotten lost, climbed a set of steps, and fallen. *Maybe Harlan?*

I scratched some more without making true headway. The writing on the wall was, I believed, something that would never be seen.

I turned my attention back to the distant beam. It looked as hopeless as it had originally, but then I noticed something hanging down from the beam. It wasn't a rope. It didn't hang straight down. Instead, it angled straight out away from me in the manner of an irregular tree limb. I could only see it in silhouette because of the light. It appeared to be maybe two inches thick throughout its length. I couldn't determine how it was secured to the beam. There was a knot of something high on the beam at the point where the object adjoined it, but I couldn't be sure if that was loose rubble or a solid connection.

Because it looked rigid I thought and hoped the hanging thing was a metal support bar that had not gone down with the rest of the ceiling. There was no way I could be sure. The bar hung down to a little below the level of my ledge. It was the only thing that I had a chance to reach, and it hung, at its closest juncture, a good ten or twelve feet from the nearest place I could stand.

It seemed to be my only hope. I was reluctant to try anything until I knew for certain how it was anchored to the beam above. I settled back and decided I'd wait for daybreak and better light. I sat for a while and then realized I'd not be able to wait. Like a clock that had not been wound, my body was running down. My right arm was throbbing. So was my head. My good shoulder was stiffening from the sap blow. My body had burned up part of the alcohol it had absorbed and that was playing havoc with my nervous system. I thought it would get worse—much worse—before it got better. I thought also that if I tried to sleep it off I'd fall off my ledge. Now and then, when I'd move, small pieces would flake off the edge or underneath of my perch and fall into the rubble below.

I stood up and turned to the door. It seemed very solid. Maybe if I kicked it repeatedly I could kick it out of its frame.

Or maybe, if I kicked a few times, my ledge would loosen and fall. Sandman and Micko would have made sure the door couldn't be opened.

If I was going to try to get out of here it had to be now, while a chance remained that my body would and could carry out demands. If I missed my jump I'd fall. The same would happen if the bar I saw turned out not to be securely attached to the beam above.

I got to my feet and did what I could to limber up protesting muscles. The ledge crumbled a little more and made some ominous noises as I did cautious exercises.

The ledge was too short and narrow to allow me to make a running jump, even if the bar was in line with the ledge, which it wasn't. I was going to have to jump flat-footed.

When my good arm and legs were as limber as I could reasonably make them, I stepped gingerly to the edge of the ledge nearest the suspended bar. I looked over the bar again. Then I flexed my muscles, took a deep breath, and sprang into the air with all the strength I had left, more a dive than a jump.

I flew and landed.

18

Friday, July 26, 3:00 A.M.

TIME SLOWED AS I hung on the bar. With my one good hand I managed to grasp the bar and lock my thighs hard around it. I'd fallen too far for my ankles to obtain purchase. The bar held, although it seemed to straighten slightly under the weight of my body. It also made an ominous squeaking noise at its upper end. But it held.

So far, so good.

My left hand, which had borne all the weight of my body in the moment before my thighs had precariously grasped the bar, had slipped down the bar a foot or so, leaving a smear of itself behind. Long years of grasping rings and high bars had allowed me to hold on. There was pain, but it was one more thing I couldn't do anything about. I tried, without much success, to ignore it.

My situation had gone from precariously deadly to dangerously deadly. I'd been an excellent gymnast in college. At that time, ten-plus years back, I'd done my routines with two sound arms and legs. Now I was hanging on a thin metal bar with one broken arm in a clumsy cast, the palm of the hand of the other scraped raw, and too little bar below to give me foot purchase.

Six months earlier I'd not have gotten this far. I'd have died on the ledge or fallen from it. Or maybe given up and dived from it.

The problem now was getting started upward. I'd worked out a plan in my head before I jumped from the ledge, but that plan had called for me catching the bar high enough to allow me to use my feet to assist in the climb. Now I hung on desperately.

I had to move higher up to use my feet. If I released my left hand grip I knew my thighs alone wouldn't hold me.

There was only one thing I could do, but at first I didn't think I was up to it. Pain is something you get used to in athletics. Exercise, done right, hurts. Accidents happen to any person who uses his body vigorously. Many times before, working on the high bar or rings, I'd pulled the skin loose from the palms of my hands. I'd also had painful sprained joints, pulled muscles, and once, a dislocated shoulder. Always before there'd been blessed time to let the injuries heal.

Not this time.

Gritting my teeth against the pain, I crossed my broken right arm across my chest, trapping the bar between the cast and my filthy shirt front. Holding the bar as tightly as I could with my right arm, I jerked and slid my left hand six inches up the bar. The pain was blinding, but I held. Then I pulled the rest of me six inches up on the bar.

On and on. I ignored the new pain in my broken arm, then ignored the pain in my injured hand. Half a foot at a time. It could not have taken more than four or five repetitions to allow me enough room to curl my feet around the bar, but it seemed to last forever.

I was finally high enough to use my thighs, calves, and feet to grip at the rust-spotted bar. I gave my hand and bad arm a tiny rest. Using my left arm to help hold my body to the bar, I managed to turn my left hand toward my face to assess the damage. I couldn't tell much. The light from the moon washed out colors, leaving all things black or in some shade of gray. There was no gray to the palm of my hand. It was black. Red looks black in the light of the moon. Blood.

My energy supply was running short, so I couldn't rest long. Already my legs were beginning to shake from the strain of supporting most of my body weight. I went back to the torture routine. Six inches up, hold, then six more inches up.

I could hear the moaning noises I made. They helped me focus diminishing strength on the task at hand.

I've no idea exactly how long I hung on and up that treacherous metal bar. I became oblivious to all except pain and the need to inch upward. The world around me ceased to be real. My senses narrowed their focus until all that existed in my universe was the two-inch metal bar I climbed. Pain became a friend. I hurt, therefore I was. Even the reason for climbing deserted me eventually, but still I climbed. I could smell only myself, the rust from the bar, and the garbage odor from the bottom of the shaft, the smell a minor part of my world.

Toward the end of the climb I know now I wasn't sane. What brought me back to reality were the cries of frustration of the organism, being myself, when there was no more bar to climb. With the return of sanity came the return of pain. I hung on the bar and screamed. I thought, for a time, that the shock to my system would drive me into unconsciousness and I would fall.

I refused to fall or lose consciousness. I regained some control, enough to allow me to assess my new situation.

I'd now reached the point where the bar adjoined the much larger metal beam. I could see it was attached to the beam by rivets or bolts and a large glob of concrete a dozen or so feet from where the beam adjoined the top of the wall I'd started from. I didn't even consider trying to get to the top of the beam. I didn't believe I could make it. Even if I was able, I believed I didn't have the balance left to benefit from the move. Maintaining such balance while crawling atop the bar seemed beyond my limited capabilities. I knew I'd have to inch my way over to the wall in the manner of a sloth, suspended below the beam by hands and legs.

Earlier, when I'd thought this part out, I'd hoped I could do it by using the crook of my left arm to support my upper body while I propelled myself along the beam with my legs.

The large hunk of concrete that lay over the area where the small bar attached itself to the beam presented a new obstacle. I disregarded it and moved, doing the two things that could be done, holding on and moving.

Pain was constant. I hooked the bend of my cast over the top of the beam and pulled myself arm over arm toward the wall until I was able to get one of my legs over the end point of the concrete hunk, which crumbled away in tiny pellets, and up over the bar.

I now journeyed over the beam and toward the wall.

Reserves inside me were on empty.

Time lost meaning again. I realized I'd reached the wall and my goal only when I banged my head hard into it. The pain of the blow was insignificant. It only served to clear my head.

I now must scramble from underneath the beam to the top of the wall of the building. I let go with my good left arm. My upper body swung slightly, but the crook of the cast stayed hooked around the beam. My upper torso was now rotated a quarter turn to the left relative to my hips and legs and my left arm hung down toward the ground. In seconds the blood rushing down into my left hand set up a searing pain strong enough to be felt above the limits of the pains already engulfing me. To fight it I brought my left hand up and touched the wall behind my head.

Ever so slowly I inched my hand along the wall behind me, turning my torso farther and farther left. A millennium later my hand found a seizable niche over the top of the wall, and one last lunging effort brought my left forearm to the top. My right arm remained hooked around the beam, the now-ragged, dirty, and disintegrating cast still reluctantly holding things in place. My upper body faced the ground. I released my legs from their grip on the beam. My lower body fell loose and slammed into the wall with a force that tried to jar my left arm loose.

All that remained was to pull all of myself up on the top of the wall where once the roof of the building had rested. I had to do that with the help of my toes. I scraped with the tip of one shoe until I found a suitable crevice. I shifted my weight to it while I did the same job with the other foot. My feet kept losing purchase, but on about the third try, I was able to throw my left leg over the wall and pull all my body after it.

For the first time since I'd leaped from the ledge, I was able to relax momentarily. I lay there, draped over the wall and the beam where it joined, and concentrated on doing nothing but breathing for a time.

I looked around cautiously. I was dizzy, but to my left sparkled the Memphis cityscape, silent now in the early morning hours. In the distance, the huge double arches of the Hernando de Soto Bridge spanned the Mississippi, curved and bright in the moonlight. From this distance I could see the lights of the few cars crossing in the early morning. A fresh breeze blew over me and the morning world smelled gloriously of exhaust fumes and river traffic.

I was exhilarated and glad to be alive. I hurt and ached all over, my clothes were ragged, my cast was dirty and coming apart, but I was alive.

Below me I saw an empty lot, littered with piles of rubble left behind when buildings that once had stood there had been demolished. Hidden beside one of the piles, out of sight of anyone not actually in the lot and up close, was my VW. I could see it from my high perch.

The other side of the wall I'd just climbed was in dark shadow, but I could make out a landing onto which my locked door evidently, at one time, had opened. For Sandman and Micko to have been able to deliver me to my ledge, there had to be steps back down.

I rested a few moments longer and then moved in the direction of the door. I straddled the wall and proceeded by scoots, checking each area of the crumbling wall top first. Soon I was above the door. I looked down again and could now make out the flight of steps descending from a landing into darkness.

If I could get down to the landing, I could crawl or walk down the stairs, get in my car, and just drive away. *Simple.*

I smiled at the thought. Only a short time before, the prospect of being able to walk away from this place had seemed like a child's dream of being loose in a sweetshop with permission to eat all. I'd been driven by desperation, by the need to try or die. But I had succeeded. I was maybe fifteen feet above my way down to freedom.

I laughed out loud. Maybe it was the alcohol.

I gave little thought to the difficulties of descending to the landing. *Piece of cake.*

I lay forward on my stomach and felt down the outside of the wall as far as I could. The outer surface was of old and uneven brick, some of them sticking out as much as an inch farther than their nearest neighbors.

I moved onto my stomach. I swung my right leg over the wall on the outside and began feeling for toeholds. I did well enough.

I was maybe halfway down to the landing before my feet slipped and my good hand pulled away.

I slid down the outer wall. I held myself tight until I hit something solid.

I stopped, found something below me to attach myself to, and fell no farther.

19

Friday, July 26, 6:45 A.M.

I CAME AWAKE this time because of bright sun in my eyes. From that sun's height I judged it was now early morning. I had aches and pains and I wondered if I could move.

But I was alive.

I'd fallen backward onto the landing. I remembered that. My legs and back had absorbed some of the shock before my head hit the weathered boards, and the landing had been large enough and sturdy enough to hold me. My good arm was locked around a landing rail, holding to it. I told the arm that all was well, but it was reluctant to follow directions and unhook itself.

I tried to get up and finally got into sitting position. I then swung my legs around so that they pointed in the direction of the steps and scooted to those steps. When my feet were resting on the second step from the top, I used my left arm to pull myself into a crouch, holding to the rail. I went down the steps like an arthritic nonagenarian. At the bottom I was, by now, sufficiently limber to get to my feet. I found an old length of two-by-four and used it for balance as I staggered to my car. The door was un-locked and I settled into the lightly padded seat. I found my key in my pocket where I'd put it after trying to scratch a message.

Time passed while I lay slumped in the seat and luxuriated in the morning heat. The garbage and junk smell was almost overwhelming.

Finally, I started the car up and drove slowly to Methodist Hospital. I was there in the emergency room for a while.

They strongly advised me to stay, but I refused. I left against medical advice.

They had reset my right arm, which, because of the strength of the cast, had not compounded. My left hand was a ball of white bandages with lonely thumb stuck out. My chest, thighs, and the insides of my upper arms were more lightly bandaged.

My clothes and shoes were in such a state of disrepair that they were fit only for garbage. But they were, for now, all I had.

It seemed stupid to return to my apartment, although I longed to go there. Someone might see me. Someone might report what they saw.

I had no money. My billfold was gone. *Drunks lose things and things are stolen from them, you know.*

I drove to Harlan's house. Driving was an adventure. I could start the car with my thumb and control the wheel some with the balled bandage. I drove slowly, hoping to see no traffic officers. I was lucky.

I made it.

The housekeeper answered the door after a time. She started to shut it when she saw me. I put my foot inside it. I was a little angry.

"Remember me, please? I was here the other day to see Harlan. I've had some bad trouble. Tell him it's Al Sears."

Her lips curled. To her I was a disheveled, disreputable, much-bandaged drunk. She nodded, finally, deciding to let someone else figure a way to get rid of me. She left me in full possession of the front door.

In a while Harlan came. I didn't know what she'd told him, but he wore a dressing gown over flowered pajamas. His right pocket showed the outline of a hand gun.

"What in hell's happened to you?"

"I just now escaped being a part of a slow urban renewal

project. Two guys, one of them Sandman Chavez, the other a guy called Micko, poured a lot of booze down me though a tube. They then left me to fall in what remains of an old building. Now I'm tired and sick and damned angry."

"You've surely been drinking," he said, realizing it. "Wilma said it, but when she gave me your name I didn't believe it."

"Listen carefully to me. They put this damned tube down my throat. I got rid of most of it. What's left has about worn off, but some stayed with me. I need something to drink, tall, cold, and lots of it."

He waited.

"A couple of big diet colas?"

"And no booze?" he asked.

"No way."

He looked me over more carefully. "I've seen some people fall hard off the wagon after taking just one drink."

"No way," I said again.

He smiled, pleased.

"And some aspirin, please." I thought for a minute. "Then, if you can spare me a place, I could stay here or get you to find me a place somewhere else. Maybe Ralph's. And Ralph needs to know I'm alive as does one other person other than you. No one else. I've got some people who think I'm dead. I want it to stay that way until I'm ready for them to know I'm alive."

"The only thing you look ready for just now is the boneyard. You can stay here. Tell me what happened."

"I got sapped. I got booze poured in me. Do you know Sandman Chavez?"

"I know him. I know who Micko is, also. The question is who hired them."

"I think I know."

"Where were you when they got you?"

I explained.

Harlan nodded wisely. "Uh-huh." He smiled gently at me. "You resemble a refugee from a death camp. I remember you in court. I used to watch you decimate prosecutors when you were at your best. You were more stubborn than they were. Sometimes owning that trait is useful."

"Yeah. What went down last night has to work in with the ongoing coin show."

"Nothing more happened last night. I've already had my morning call from my men at the show. But only about half the dealers were there last night. Lots who didn't make it last night were on your numbers list. I've got a lot of men around that place. I put some technicians inside early this morning to do special wiring and cameras. Got them dressed in maintenance uniforms. We're keeping things looking like normal."

"It will be tonight or tomorrow night."

"I'll believe you until it turns out different. If you want you can be with me both nights, watching. How about a gun?"

"Maybe. If I can manage to shoot one. I can't just now."

He shrugged, not caring.

"You need clothes." He looked me over. "I've got some stuff from my younger, thinner days that might fit. God, you're a mess."

I wasn't satisfied with his attitude. "There are going to be a bunch of men running around your coin show with Uzis and a box or two of dynamite. I'd like you to counter with a howitzer and maybe a battalion of Marines."

"The Marines would be in the way. Trust me on this one, Al. Forget you were once a lawyer and I was once a cop. Remember that I'm now no longer a cop. Believe, even if it seems fanciful to you, that I can deal with dynamite and Uzis. I no longer have to read anyone their rights, and I don't need to get search warrants. I don't need a judge or a prosecutor to go along with me and mine."

He saw I was still not convinced and shook his head. When he began again his voice was lower.

"Remember that worldwide convention of judges here in Memphis last year?"

I nodded. I did remember.

"There were threats. Some people slipped into the country

from South America. Some were sent by the Cubans, some by the Colombians. There were nine men who came. They had plastic explosives and automatic weapons. It was intended to be a bloody mess."

"I never heard about any mess."

"There wasn't one. We took them out up front."

"What happened to them? I saw nothing in the papers."

"Sometime, I'll tell you, but for now it's nothing you need to know."

"Doesn't sound legal, Harlan."

He smiled and I smiled.

"Legal is as legal does. The world has become illegal, Al. Your law's become a laugh. It makes it easy for bastards. So did mine when I was a twenty-year-plus cop. It isn't that way for me now."

ON FRIDAY, ALL the long night, stiff, sick, and sore, I sat with Harlan and two of his people in the back of an old, nondescript Ford U-Haul truck. The right front tire of the truck was picturesquely flat. Television screens inside the truck gave us views of both the outside of the building housing the coin show and of some spots in the garden area between the exhibition hall and the motel. Two inside fixed cameras gave a panoramic view of the bourse area itself.

"Won't they spot the inside cameras?"

"They'd see normal cameras, which go dark when the bourse closes. The new ones we installed are more difficult to spot. And the outside ones are hidden in trees and set up on top of buildings near the hall rather than on the hall, itself. The inside ones look like light fixtures," Harlan explained patiently. "Even if you were suspicious you'd not know you were being watched without inspecting things very closely. Watch inside the show with me. See if you can spot anything or anyone who looks familiar."

I saw many familiar people. I saw dozens of customers who came to Ralph's shop. I saw Ace and Deuce at their table. I saw Ralph. Harlan had contacted him for me. He knew I was safe and in hiding. I'd contacted Sue myself and promised to call her again in the morning.

I drank buckets of coffee and diet cola through the night. I found I was still slightly affected by the forced-down liquor. It wasn't a true hangover, but hangover was the closest way it could be described. My body was used to a lot of alcohol or no alcohol at all. I guessed it didn't know exactly how to react to a moderate dose. The headache had vanished. My broken arm didn't ache as much as it had when I'd arrived at Harlan's house, just after they'd recast it. My left palm was scabbing over. I'd removed most of its bandage when I'd given myself a needed bath. I could now aim and awkwardly point a gun, raw index finger laid along the barrel. Twelve hours of sleep and some food had helped immensely. I was still sore, and parts of me hurt where I never remembered hurting before.

Friday night got over without incident. It became Saturday morning. A thin rain fell on the streets.

"They'll come tonight," I said.

Harlan nodded. "Could it be something else?"

"No," I said, positive of it.

"Okay, okay," he said, resigned to my fanaticism.

"Tell Ralph to close early tonight. Tell him to go home and lock himself in upstairs."

"I thought you were sure."

"I'm sure."

"We'll leave Ralph alone, then. He leaves early, maybe someone would notice because it isn't in his nature to pull out early. I told him to go through the motions about you. If anyone asked he was to say you'd probably fallen off the wagon. I told him he was to act unsurprised and also disgusted. He told me to tell you that your ex-wife had called. He made a deal with her on the chain cent. He said, during the deal, that she asked a lot of questions about you."

I smiled, not caring.

• • •

WE WENT BACK to Harlan's house for the day. The maid fixed us first-class ham and biscuits and gravy. She had begun to smile at me now that I was clean and wearing Harlan's old clothes. I told Harlan that I might marry her and take her away from his plantation.

He smiled painfully.

What I'd said to him reminded me to call Sue again.

"Last night was quiet. I think this all will finish tonight. I'll see you then. And remember, you don't know where I am. You've not seen me or heard from me."

"You'll come here when it's done?"

"Yes."

"There's still Judy."

"Forget Judy," I said.

"Have you forgotten her?"

"Please believe that I have. And that's after a very close encounter with her and her new boyfriend. Part of my problems that you have yet to witness are from that meeting."

"Tell me what you mean."

"Later," I said. "Late tonight. Early tomorrow morning. I double promise. And you're my full-time, all-time girl if you'll have me."

"Okay," she said. She laughed a little. "Okay."

I slept after breakfast. I awoke once, but the house seemed quiet and the sun, from my window, was high overhead. I slept some more. When I got up I made one more phone call. I called Willie Farr. Red answered the phone.

"Willie ain't here, Al. He had to go out on his tax business. He left one message for you. He ran down your Clement Johnson. He's back in prison and has been there for a couple of months."

"Thanks, Red. I appreciate the information. Tell Willie I said thanks. And don't say anything to anyone about talking to me. Some people believe I'm dead."

"Whatever," he said. "Willie said this morning that it sure is funny quiet around this old river town."

"Yeah."

"Willie also said it was peculiar quiet."

IT WAS AFTER dark when we went back to the truck. The television screens were turned on. The pictures that came back to us weren't quite true. It was like seeing yourself in one of those mirrors shopkeepers install to watch for shoplifters.

At closing time the coin collectors moved out the door. Things got less hectic inside. Lights were lowered. Dealers stashed thick wads of cash inside their display cases, locked the flimsy locks, covered up the cases, and followed the collectors outside.

"There's a man under that table," Harlan said, pointing out a table in the bourse area near the wall.

"I didn't see him hide," I said, upset at missing it.

"You were watching the crowd coming out. I was watching for someone staying inside. He went under that closed table about half an hour ago. He was pretty quick, but I was watching the spot because the dealer who has the table has a name cloth covering it that almost touches the floor. The guy under the table has some kind of two-way radio." He yawned. "It will be a while yet. My bet is they'll wait until things get late and quiet at the motel. Two or three in the morning." He gave me a satisifed look, pleased with me.

"How many men will you have inside?" I asked.

"Four, for a while. That's usual. The four inside know what to do and when. We're in radio contact with them also."

I waited and watched. Nothing happened. It was hard to stay awake.

At just before three in the morning an eighteen-wheel semi-truck pulled in the big lot and parked three spots away from us. Men scrambled out of the semi, front and back. The outside cameras didn't pick them up well, but I counted six of them. The driver stayed in his cab. *Five, plus one in the cab, and one inside the coin show. Maybe more inside the trailer.*

One man, who carried a large, newspaper-wrapped package,

walked to the river side of the building. There was a security shack back there, but it was unlighted and deserted. I saw him check inside it. He turned and waved to the others. I recognized him, *Sandman Chavez*. He moved toward the river, watching around him.

The other four went out of our television picture. When they reappeared there were still four, but one of the four was bound and gagged and was being carried.

"Night bellman," Harlan said softly to me. "They've put one of their own out front of the motel now."

The group of men moved toward a window that opened from the exhibit hall out into a garden. One of them lifted a handheld radio. He pressed a button on it.

"Recognize anyone?"

"One of those could be Micko. I never got a real good look at more than his sap."

"One is Micko. The thick one in the dark sweater."

"Sandman went toward the river."

"I saw that."

We waited and watched while the three men in the garden area donned ski masks. They deposited the fourth man in a convenient corner and left him laying there.

When the explosion came I was only partially set for it. I jumped as it rocked our vehicle. I could see fire and smoke on one of our outdoor screens, the one which showed a part of the back of the motel. The motel itself went completely dark. Our screens all remained lighted, power on.

"He set off a small package of dynamite sticks against the big pole that held the transformer," Harlan said matter-of-factly. "I'd guess that would be for diversion and to keep things in an uproar inside the motel." He nodded to himself. "Watch the men in the garden area."

I watched. I also tried to see what was happening inside the bourse area. It was very dark. The cameras inside could pick up very little in the absence of light. I wondered what had happened to Harlan's inside guards. And then I saw them. Four of them.

They were now outside the building, moving into the trees that bordered the parking area.

Two intruders in the garden area took out large black plumber's helpers and attached them to the large window. Either it had been earlier cut inside or it was weak because they plucked the window away.

The men went swiftly through the created opening. I saw their ugly guns glint against the half-light.

"Now they're inside and our guards have escaped to the outside," Harlan said laconically. "Keep watching the garden area."

A man appeared and I recognized him as one of Harlan's. He picked up the semi-conscious night porter in a fireman's hold and carried him out of my view.

"They're now inside thinking about collecting the money. They're wondering where the guards went and that has them a little upset."

Near us I heard the motor of the semi that had brought the robbers start up. There were several dozen reports, shots of some kind.

"That will be your headman-planner and his driver. Kind of chicken on their parts. The driver stayed with the cab, the head man's inside the trailer. But they just got a worried radio report from the bourse and were going to motor out. I put a couple of sharpshooters around and they blew out all eighteen tires." He listened intently. From far away I could hear sirens. "And coming now, a bit late, but never too late, are our good friends in blue. Three or four minutes away. Enough time to clean things up."

I saw some of Harlan's men on the roof of the motel. They were guarding the opening that the intruders had made in the glass window. Two of the watchers were armed with automatic weapons, big ones. Rifles, not pistols.

"My lead man on that roof can shoot the eye out of a squirrel at fifty yards," Harlan said. He flipped a switch. He took a microphone from a wall bracket.

"Attention inside the building. You're surrounded. We've shot out all the tires on your escape truck. You're all alone inside the exhibition area. If you try to exit with weapons our sharpshooters will be waiting for you and will shoot you on sight. Throw out your weapons. Remove your ski masks. You are allowed to exit only at the main door of the exhibition center. Come out with your hands held high in the air."

One man tried the garden exit. He started bravely and wildly out with his Uzi held high. He fired a stutter burst up into the sky at the roof. He was down before he got two steps from the window. He lay unmoving.

Another tried a back door. A fusillade of shots drove him back inside. I saw him dimly in the interior monitors. Someone had turned on a flashlight. He limped back to the others. They fell into argument.

One stripped off his mask, and then a second. Then all discarded weapons and walked to the exhibition hall door. I saw it open. They came out.

The one who'd taken the night employee's place came into my view under separate guard.

Sandman didn't appear for a long time. When he did appear he was wet.

"He tried to swim for it," Harlan said, smiling. "We had two boats out there. One of them got him." He nodded. "Very satisfactory. The driver is out and caught. That's all of them except for the one in the truck trailer."

I thought of something. "Best keep your men away from the trailer."

Harlan raised his eyebrows.

"There's sure to be more dynamite inside the trailer. I don't think it would happen, but he might decide to take some people along with him. Stay back a little and let him make his own decision after thinking about it."

Harlan nodded. He gave terse instruction over the radio. Men near the eighteen wheeler pulled back. Someone turned a spotlight on the opened rear doors of the trailer.

"Wait another few minutes and then let me talk with him," I said.

"Okay. Your play, Al." He watched me for a long moment. "I'd like to know who you think is in that trailer?"

I told him and he nodded.

"I can talk to him if you'd rather," he said.

"No."

"You could get up close and he could blow himself to hell along with you."

"No. I'll wait another minute. He's had a chance to think on suicide. And I'll stand a little away from the truck. If I can work a gun I'll aim a couple of random shots through the back doors."

I used the mike. "Come out. Come out of the trailer now. If you don't then I'll fire two warning shots. Then all these guards will fire. Come out without a weapon."

I moved outside and to within fifty feet or so from the truck. The back doors were open and it was dark inside. I figured if the occupant set off a big jolt of dynamite it would likely end me along with him. I was angry enough not to care.

More light came from another new spotlight. I could see part of the inside of the trailer.

I lifted the pistol and fired two shots in through the doors of the trailer. The pistol made soft bangs. A .22. I fired high, but the shots hit off the steel ceiling and richocheted wildly. The gun stung my hand.

"Stop shooting," a voice called. "I'm coming out."

He did.

Harlan stood next to me. He was smiling.

The man came down out of the truck. A couple of Harlan's people checked him for weapons and then let him join his defeated army. Sandman watched and waited with the same group.

I walked near.

"Hi, boys," I said companionably.

Sandman shook his head. "Damned cat."

The brains of the outfit wouldn't look at me.

Duke.

186

20

Friday, August 23, 8:00 P.M.

ABOUT A MONTH later Harlan and Ralph jointly threw a party for me. It was to celebrate both my new employment and Sue's and my engagement. A lot of people came: lawyers who'd known me and not completely shunned me after I was suspended, some men and women working for insurance companies and banks I'd done jobs for as a PI, coin friends, and even some coin dealers who'd been prominent on the "hit" list. Willie and Red came and sat nearby where I sat, and I talked to them for a while, liking them both a lot. Now and then Red would salute me with a bottle, but the room was air-conditioned and I saw Willie shivering. They left early.

I smiled at all of the guests, but the only person I really saw was Sue. She wore her new, red dress. She was bright and bubbly and she also wore the diamond I'd given her, third finger, left hand.

Judy was there accompanied by her new husband, Robbins Whitehead. His once-swollen face had returned to mere sullen pompousness, which was normal. He looked portly and harried. He smiled happily at me and my broken arm and said nothing about either a Porsche or a shovel. I let it go at that.

Judy came because her television station had sent her to cover my party. The foiled robbery attempt had been the biggest sum- mer news so far for Memphis. The amount of possible loot in- volved, the audacity of the plan, and the way it had been prevented, had caught the imagination of Memphis and a lot of the country on a slack news weekend. My part in same, as I was shown bandaged and broken, had been retold wrong by CBS, ABC, NBC, and the rest a dozen times. *Sixty Minutes* had called. A group of area legislators had publicly proposed that my sus- pension be immediately lifted. I'd refused comment. When I'd been interviewed I'd lowered my voice, shifted my feet, refused to look straight into the cameras, and generally been a news problem. I'd given all of the credit to Harlan and company. Many of the stories had then become concerned with Harlan and firm, once I'd proved to be a reluctant and colorless hero.

The publicity was working well for business. That was fine, because Harlan was my new boss.

I'd vacillated until the bandages came off. Ralph had urged me to take the proffered job. It was more money, more respon- sibility. He'd said I could come back to coins and part-time in- vestigating if things failed to work out. He also said he could hire someone else for less money and that the new someone might split an order of fries, rather than declining same because of a ru- ined digestive tract.

So I was now Harlan's executive assistant, for whatever that title meant. So far the way it had worked was that I did things in Harlan's stead while he stayed home and spent more time with his wife and, perhaps, also tried to keep things peaceful with his housekeeper.

The job had been interesting. I thought I was going to be able to do it. I was hoping when the cast came off my arm I'd get to spend some time away from the office, doing what needed doing in faraway places. That was still two weeks away.

But already, a couple of times, I'd found that my earlier life of defending persons accused of crime had made me aware of what the criminal mind might plan and how to guard against same.

The party was at the Peabody Hotel. The ballroom was the

rental site. There weren't any speeches, just a lot of friends, plus a trio of musicians playing on the stage. There was good food and strong drinks for those in attendance.

I drank iced tea.

Once I saw Judy glancing darkly at me as I danced awkwardly with Sue. The moment was not unsweet. Dancing was difficult for me to do with an arm still in a cast, but I managed a flourish or two, showing off, watching Judy burn.

Judy had also brought a man from her television station with her. He carried a portable camera and liked to lift it, turn on bright lights, and blind the beholders. Once, when that was happening, Judy asked me a question or two in her best, soft voice.

"How are you feeling now, Al?"

"All right, Judy."

"Do you know anything about a trial date?"

"No." I looked dumb and unconcerned about such things and I could see I was making her furious. I knew when the trial date was and so did she.

"There's a lot of talk around here and Nashville that your suspension will be lifted. If it is will you go back to practicing law?"

"I don't know. I don't need to be repaid for doing something I was supposed to do." I gave her my best "aw shucks" look, the one that had eventually turned off the networks.

"I'm sure you feel that way," she said warmly, although her eyes were still cold. I wondered if Judy would confide to her big crowd of night watchers that we'd once been married. If she did there was always a chance that Robbins would return with his shovel. Late in the evening I looked over at their table and they were arguing, while the cameraman stood politely away. They left soon after that without saying good-bye. Maybe it was because of time problems with the late news. Maybe it was because Judy had spent a lot of her time talking warmly to the youngest member of the musical trio.

By midnight the crowd was down to Ralph, Harlan and his beautiful wife, and Sue and me at our table. The trio quit playing music, packed up, and left us in quiet. Now and then someone from the Peabody management would come to the door to see if we were still there.

"Go through it once more for me, Al? How you figured it?" Ralph asked. He'd been drinking Heinekens and it has extra alcohol, as I once well knew. He was pleasantly along. I was still an expert on how intoxicated someone was.

I took a salad fork and drew an imaginary line on the table cloth. "At first I thought it was Harlan. No kidding, I really did. I got a snake dropped in my car at his place. And he was present when your poker party got invaded, Ralph. Plus Harlan ran the company with the contract to guard the coin show."

Harlan looked amused. He hadn't smiled that much when I first told him my story, but now he smiled. My suspicions then had become funny to him now.

"Ralph convinced me it wasn't you, Harlan. Then I got almost sure it was Abraham Burks. There were enough zillions of dollars to interest anyone, even someone like Abe. He knew something about coins from Millie, his vanished wife. He'd tagged behind her to coin shops and maybe some coin shows. He had to know that coin shows, in total, were worth big money. But it seemed not to be his kind of caper. Abe already has money. Having it has made life dangerous for him. He stays hidden behind fences, guarded by men and dogs. It was a chore to get in when I went to see him. And Abe has at least one very tough man working for him. If Abe had wanted me dead, anytime, then I guess I'd likely have died."

Sue put her small hand in mine. I patted it reassuringly before continuing.

"I thought it could be Abe because I'd represented his wife and he was afraid something about her would still come out. And so the raid on Ralph's poker party." I shook my head. "I believe Abe about Millie and so do the police, now." I'd not told anyone about my adventure over the fence into Abe's estate. I'd let the police and the world assume Sandman and Micko had caught me as I'd walked back from my watch on Abe's entranceway. "Abe looked for me when he was looking for Millie. He looked casually, not hard. When he didn't find me easily he gave up. It wasn't the way of a man who was afraid I could pass something on that I knew about him."

"What do you believe happened to Abe's wife, Sherlock?" Harlan asked.

"I'm not completely certain. Maybe no one will ever find out, maybe she'll turn up. She took her gold coins when she left Abe's house that last day. That means to me that she didn't plan on returning afterward. The police are talking to Ace and Deuce about Millie. They were selling her coins when she assembled the set, either selling them to her or locating them for her. I thought if she was running, and in the mood to sell them back for escape money, that she'd have tried to use the two of them to get rid of at least a part of the coins. So far Ace and Deuce keep saying no. They swear she didn't come to them when she left Abe's house."

"Do you believe them?" Ralph asked.

"No, not all the way. I don't like them and neither do you. Neither of us wanted them here tonight. I think they might have stolen Millie's gold if they could have done the job easily. But they know who Abe is. Knowing him makes me doubt they'd blatantly steal from his wife. My feeling's reinforced by the fact they still deal in junk and live poor. But maybe they could know something. I think they introduced her to the main man in this thing. It was probably casual, but they put her onto Duke and Duke onto her."

"Are you saying she ran off with her gold to be with Duke?"

"Could be. It might be possible to find out. I have a list of the gold coins she took with her. If Millie did meet Duke and fall hard, then she fell when Duke was figuring out the the biggest thieving deal he'd ever considered. I think he started theorizing on it a long time back. I believe he got out of coins so he'd be less suspect. He sold Ralph his stuff before I went to work at the shop. The people interested might try to find a buyer that Duke maybe sold Millie's gold to, if it comes to that. Ralph could help by putting the list on the teletype. But so far Millie's disappearance is unsolved." I shook my head. "And if it gets down to that I know someone who'd pursue it if the police totally lose interest."

"Abe?" Harlan asked.

I nodded.

"Why did Duke send someone after you and me?" Ralph asked.

"I was a problem for him. You weren't. The killer who came to your poker party just had carte blanche. He may have been in your shop, taken there by our dead pal, Benny. He knew there was stuff worth stealing downstairs." I nodded. "But I had to go. I knew Duke. I knew things about him that would make me automatically suspect him if a coin show robbery went down. And I was no longer his lawyer. I'd surely pass my suspicions on to you and the world. So I had to go up front of the coin show robbery." I looked inquiringly at Ralph. "Remember when I first showed you that scrap of paper with Benny's list of numbers on it?"

"I remember."

"Your number was on it. If you got robbed you and I would surely have talked about it. I'd tell you things about Duke that I know. I'd tell you, in Duke's thinking, about things that he'd believed were privileged communications when I was a lawyer. I'd not have told you anything that was privileged, but Duke thought I would. So I got to be worth a big-time contract. When that didn't work, he spent some little time trying to talk me into leaving Memphis. If I'd have taken him up on that I've a gut feeling that I might never have made it back to old Memphis town. Duke's a devious man. He likes planning rather than direct action. He tried the snake and got frustrated when that didn't work. So he ordered the toughest two of his people to follow me, drown me in alcohol, and drop me off a wall. It was to look accidental. Because he had a taste for the devious he considered and ordered a devious man, Sandman, to help him out."

Harlan smiled. "Sandman's still talking, in jail, about you getting down from that place. He thinks you're some kind of superman who can fly out of a high, lonely place. I halfway agree. I went to that godforsaken building while you were sleeping in my house that first morning. I found it. I went up those steps and looked inside at your perch and the steel rod and beam. I can't believe it happened like it did. I've hope you'll continue to surprise me." He thought for a moment. "And so you figured it was Duke?"

"Yes. I thought about everyone. Duke was only an included in the list at first. I checked down my own past. Duke had his gun at the poker party. He's not a gunman. He's a schemer. Why the gun? And why'd he bother to come to your poker party at all after he'd quit coins. My guess is he was curious. He wanted to see the way things went down. And being on the scene could help him avoid suspicion."

"And Benny?" Ralph asked.

"Benny got killed within hours of the attempt at the poker party. I was never real sure, until Sandman had me, why Benny got killed. He got killed because he somehow obtained the table numbers where the dealers would be located. Maybe he stole them, maybe he just found them out, but my bet is he found them out because Duke paid him for them. Benny maybe then wanted a little off the top. My guess is he asked for something more than minor payment. His sister said he was nervous and watchful before he got whacked. Duke bought the numbers from Benny, so Benny was going to die. Sandman and Micko told me, knowing I was soon to be a dead man, that Micko beat Benny to death with a sap. It was just good economics and sense to get rid of Benny. Once the robbery went down Benny would have been like a bug on a griddle. He'd have either talked or looked so guilty that someone would have gotten the whole story out of him in minutes. But, for another thing that made me figure it, remember the scrap of paper with the list of numbers and something else on it, Ralph?"

"That doodling?"

"To you and me it was that. But then, thinking on it, it looked just a little like a coronet, a crown, or a coat of arms of some kind. Duke is caught up in that sort of thing. He reads books on aristocracy, he talks royalty, he even buys his drinking glasses with crowns and coronets on them." I looked all around the table and smiled. "What royal personage, famous in fact and fable, allowed herself to be bitten by a snake and so died?"

"Cleopatra," Sue said.

"Sure. So I park my car next to the zoo. Duke then had the idea and the chance to drop a poisonous snake inside. He was watching and waiting and getting more and more desperate to do me in. And because I'd once helped him to stay out of jail, maybe he'd decided I deserved a noble death. I knew Sandman and Micko hadn't thought of or arranged the snake thing because, when they had me, they kept talking about the boss having taken the blame for the snake fiasco. Duke somehow knew about the zoo and what was going on there. He could have read it in the paper or seen something on evening television. Judy told me she had a story about the fire at the zoo and the shutdown there."

"How could this Duke person have arranged to put a snake in your car in the time you were in our house? How would he have known you were there? Were you followed?" Harlan's wife asked.

"I didn't think I was followed. Maybe I was," I said vaguely.

"No," Harlan said. He looked at his wife with a softness I'd never seen for anyone else. "Al's being a nice guy. I was to blame, if there was blame. Duke was in my office the morning I got the call on the Arizona note. He called and came in, ostensibly to tell me the same kind of stuff he'd tried to lay on Al. From hearing my side of the phone conversation he knew Al would be at my house later in the morning. All he had to do was go out from our house, remember about the zoo, steal the snake, and wait. He could have managed it in a lot less time than what was available."

We'd talked privately about this before and I knew about it, but I didn't want Harlan's wife to feel that anything had gone wrong that Harlan might have caused.

Call it job protection.

I continued on swiftly. "There were tens of millions in coins involved. Some of the bandits who got picked up are now talking, trying to make their own separate deals. Smitty told Harlan

194